Witch Is When
It All Began

Published by Implode Publishing Ltd
© Implode Publishing Ltd 2015

Chapter 1

"What's that *thing*?" The young man looked horrified.

"That's Winky."

How dare he call my darling cat a *thing*? Sure, Winky had only one eye, and looked as though he'd just walked off the set of a slasher movie, but deep down, underneath all that fur and latent aggression, he was sweet and adorable. At least, that's what the woman at the cat re-homing centre had told me. Gullible? Who? Me?

Winky jumped onto my desk, and immediately the young man pushed his chair back. He probably thought he'd be safe at that distance, but he hadn't seen how far Winky could jump.

"Get down!" I tried to push Winky off the desk, but he managed to avoid my arm. His meowing grew louder as he walked around in circles, directing his attention first at me and then at the young man. "Sorry about this." I forced a smile, and pressed the intercom. "Mrs V?"

"Hello." Mrs V's voice crackled through.

"Mrs V, can you come — ?"

"Hello?"

Mrs V was my PA/receptionist. At least, that was her official job title, but in reality she was more 'knitter-in-residence'. She spent most of her time churning out scarves. Lots of them. She was also a little deaf.

"Excuse me for a moment." I got up and made my way to the outer office.

"Mrs V!"

"I thought I heard you on the intercom," she said. Her finger was still pressed on the 'talk' button.

"Would you come and take Winky? I think he needs feeding."

"You know I hate that cat."

That was the understatement of the decade. Mrs V and Winky did not see eye-to-eye, and that had nothing to do with his deficiency in the ocular department. She wasn't really a 'cat person'.

"Please," I pleaded. Got to let her know who's the boss. "Just until I've finished with this client."

"What about my yarn? You know what that cat's like."

The large mail sack, which was wedged between two filing cabinets, was full to bursting with balls of wool of every colour and type known to man. Some people collect stamps, some people collect coins, Mrs V collected yarn. It was a compulsion; she couldn't help herself. Wherever she went, she had to buy more.

Winky would have had a field day in that sack. He'd ransacked it once before, and on that occasion, I'd only just managed to convince Mrs V not to toss him out of the window.

"I'll move the sack into the corridor," I offered.

"Someone might steal my yarn if you put it out there," she protested. Her concern was no doubt fuelled by the high number of yarn thefts in the area.

"It'll be safe. I promise."

"Oh, all right then." She didn't sound convinced. "But I don't understand why you can't take that stupid cat home with you. He makes the office smell."

I'd no intention of taking Winky back to my flat. It was the one place I had any peace and quiet. And besides, I didn't want a one-eyed cat wrecking my love life—not that I had one. But I lived in hope.

Mrs V walked over to my desk, smiled at the young man, and then grabbed Winky by the scruff of the neck, like a mother cat lifting its young. Except that Winky didn't think of Mrs V as his mother. They were sworn enemies. Winky thrashed about, meowing and spitting at her.

"Sorry about that," I said, once the room was clear of both cat and mad knitting lady.

"What happened to its eye?" the young man asked.

"I don't know. It was already like that when I got him from the cat re-homing centre. I felt sorry for him because he looked so sad." It turned out that psycho looked an awful lot like sad. "Anyway, how can I help you?"

"I was expecting—" The young man hesitated. "You're not Ken Gooder."

No flies on this guy.

"I'm *Jill* Gooder. Ken was my father. He died three years ago."

"Oh, I'm sorry. The sign outside still has his name on it."

"I haven't got around to changing it yet."

"Are you a private investigator?"

"P.I. born and bred, that's me. How can I help?"

It was usually about now that the would-be client remembered an urgent appointment: dentist, doctor, optician—I'd heard them all. The best excuse I'd heard so far had been from the guy who'd remembered an urgent chiropodist appointment—some kind of ingrown toenail emergency. Even in the age of so-called equality, a lot of people—mainly men—refused to believe that a woman was capable of being a P.I. That was the reason I hadn't changed the sign—it got the punters through the door.

Once they were inside, I had to persuade them I was up to the job. I'd joined my father's business straight from school, but I'd mostly worked in the background. I wasn't much of a 'people person' — at least not according to my sister, Kathy. Since my father's death, I'd had no choice but to work on my 'customer-facing' skills. *Customer-facing?* Who comes up with this rubbish?

The young man hesitated. He was probably deciding which medical excuse to go with. My money was on the optician.

"What's your name?" I asked. If I could keep him talking, there was still hope.

"Danny. Danny Peterson."

He was the type of guy I found difficult to pin an age on. Twenty-three? Maybe. But he could just as easily have been thirty-three. Good looking, I guess, but not really my type. *'My type'?* Who was I kidding? If my track record was anything to go by, 'my type' was a lying, cheating, unreliable narcissist.

"So what can I do for you today, Danny?" I flashed him my best *customer-facing* smile.

"It's my girlfriend. She—" Tears began to well in his eyes.

What was I supposed to do now? I wasn't good around people when they cried — especially not men. Kathy was the empathetic one in our family.

"Are you okay? Would you like a tissue?" I hoped not because I'd run out the day before, and had been using toilet roll.

"Sorry. I didn't mean to—," he whimpered.

"That's okay. Did something happen to your girlfriend?"

"She was murdered."

Oh bum. I hadn't seen that one coming. I'd more or less assumed he suspected her of cheating on him. I got a lot of that type of work: unfaithful husbands, wives, boyfriends and girlfriends. It was enough to destroy your faith in human nature—assuming you had any in the first place. I took on a lot of missing-persons cases too. I preferred those, although most of the time the 'missing' person turned out not to be missing at all.

Murder cases? Not so many. In fact, since my father died, I'd had precisely—none.

"We were going to get engaged." Danny had managed to stem the tears, which was just as well because the economy toilet roll was particularly rough. Times were hard in the P.I. business. "Look." He took a small, red box out of his jacket pocket. "This is the ring."

"Very nice." I was no expert on jewellery, but I figured the solitaire had probably set him back a few hundred pounds. "I assume the police are already involved?"

"Yes, but they're useless. They won't listen to me."

In my line of business, I frequently came into contact with the local Washbridge police. We had a kind of love/hate relationship. I hated them, and they loved to hate me. My dad had enjoyed a much better working relationship with them. I put it down to the fact that I'm a woman, and they were all chauvinist scum-bags. According to Kathy, it was more likely to be because I was opinionated and difficult to get along with. According to her, I didn't have an ounce of tact. That simply wasn't true. It wasn't my fault that they were all incompetent asshats.

"Are the police treating you as a suspect?"

"No, of course not. They know I didn't have anything to

do with it. They just won't accept that Caroline's murder was the work of a serial killer."

"And you think it was?" As far as I was aware, Washbridge had never had a serial killer.

"I'm sure of it. Hey, could you pull down the blinds?" The sun had broken through the clouds, and Danny had to shield his eyes in order to see me.

"They're stuck I'm afraid. Try shuffling the chair a few inches that way."

The large window behind me was divided into three panes. The central blind was stuck in the 'down' position. The two outer blinds were stuck half open, half closed. They'd been that way for years. Normally something like that would have driven me insane, but I didn't like to make changes to the office, not even the faulty blinds, because it reminded me of Dad. I might not be most people's idea of a P.I., but at least my office looked the part. Dad had styled it on those old detective movies of the fifties and sixties. It was the sort of office that Sam Spade would have been proud to own. Kathy was always telling me to get the office modernised, but I wouldn't hear of it. I loved it the way it was—even the creaking floorboards.

"What makes you think that your girlfriend was murdered by a serial killer?"

"I don't *think* she was; I *know* she was. Her name was Caroline Fox."

I waited for more information, but he seemed to have rested his case. It was as if her name alone should have had some kind of significance. Was she famous? I didn't really keep up-to-date with the culture of celebrity—that was more Kathy's department. I rarely watched TV, and much preferred to read a good book. Maybe his girlfriend was someone I should have heard of?

"Caroline Fox?"

"Don't you see? Her name was Fox."

It was only nine-thirty, and I was never at my best in the morning, but it felt like I was missing something.

"Sorry. I'm not sure what you're getting at."

He looked at me as though I was thicker than the solid wooden desk that separated us.

"The Animal!" he said, with no attempt to hide his exasperation.

"Animal?" Why was he speaking in riddles?

"Don't you read the news?"

"Not often." I rarely bothered because it was always so depressing.

"It was all over the 'Bugle'."

The Bugle was the local rag, which wasn't exactly renowned for its cutting-edge journalism. It was sensationalist by nature, and rarely bothered to fact check its stories. All in all, it was a bit of a joke.

"You're going to have to give me more," I said.

Danny sighed. What little faith he may have had in me was slowly ebbing away.

"There were two other murders. The first was just over two months ago. Her name was Lyon. Not long after that, another woman was murdered. Her name was Lamb. Now do you see?"

"You think they were murdered because they had an 'animal' surname?"

"It isn't just me who thinks so."

"The Bugle?"

"Yes! They ran a story on 'The Animal' serial killer."

"What do the police think about it?"

"They insist it's just a coincidence. They won't take it seriously because, strictly speaking, the first victim's name wasn't an animal."

"I thought you said her name was Lion."

"It was, but it was spelled L Y O N."

"Maybe they're right. Maybe it is just a coincidence."

"I don't believe it. The victims' names were Lyon, Lamb and Fox. How can that be a coincidence?"

"Stranger things have happened." Trust me on this one.

"Will you help me or not?" Danny said.

Business was slow—very slow. Like 'where's the rent coming from?' slow. I was faced with a dilemma. Dad would never have taken on a case unless he genuinely thought he could help. He'd always insisted we had professional standards to maintain. Yeah well—sorry Dad—I needed the cash.

"Of course. I'll be happy to help."

After Danny had left, I checked the online archive of the Bugle. It didn't take long to bring myself up to speed. Pauline Lyon's murder had been front page news. The article had included a description of a man spotted near the murder scene, and an artist's impression of a tattoo on the man's left arm—two daggers through a heart. A few days later they had printed an appeal for more witnesses to come forward. Not long after that, another front page article had reported the murder of Trisha Lamb. The serial killer theory hadn't occurred to the Bugle's esteemed journalists until a week later when it ran the infamous 'The Animal' headline. This final article seemed half-baked and poorly researched. I could understand why the police had given it little weight.

Chapter 2

"How's business?" Kathy asked when I called in at her place for our regular 'catch-up'.

"Slow." I sighed. "Like slower than a sloth on a slow day."

Kathy was twenty nine; four years older than me. We were nothing like one another in terms of appearance or personality. That was hardly surprising because I was adopted when I was a baby. Mum and Dad had told me as soon as I was old enough to understand. They treated Kathy and me just the same, so I never gave the whole adoption thing much thought until I turned eighteen. I'd been worried how Mum and Dad might react when I told them that I wanted to trace my birth parents. Not only did they encourage me, they even helped with all the paperwork. It turned out to be a waste of time because my birth father was unknown, and my birth mother refused to see me. That had really hurt. I'd had this idea that my birth mother was waiting for me to get in touch, and that we'd have this fantastic reunion. When she rejected me for a second time, Mum and Dad were there for me again. They understood how much that second rejection had hurt. It still did.

"You need to change the sign, and invest in some marketing," Kathy said.

"I will. I promise."

Did I mention that my sister was the bossy one? Oh yeah! Miss Bossy Boots—that was Kathy. When we were kids, she'd always been the one who decided which game to play or which clothes to dress up in. Now, she spent endless hours trying to organise my business, and my love life. Good luck with that one. Still, I loved her to bits. We'd always been close, and especially so since we lost Mum and Dad. Even though she had her own family now, she still had time for me.

"*When* are you going to change it?"

See what I mean? Bossy.

"Soon. Anyway, I have a new case I'm working on."

"Is it a juicy one?"

"You know I can't tell you." I take my professional standards very seriously.

"Go on. Tell me."

"Oh, all right then." Maybe not all that seriously. "It's a murder. The victim's boyfriend came to see me. He thinks it's the work of a serial killer."

"That does sound juicy. Makes a change from unfaithful husbands. Tell me more."

"There isn't much to tell. He only came to see me yesterday. Do I get a cup of tea?"

"Can't you tell me about the case first?"

"Tea first."

"Come into the kitchen then." She sighed. Kathy hated it when I got the upper-hand. "You can fill me in while I make tea. Watch out for the Lego."

Kathy's house was a disaster zone. She had two kids: Mikey was seven and Lizzie was almost five. Although they were out at school, you could see where they'd been. I loved my niece and nephew to bits, but if I wanted to have a grown-up conversation, I had to visit while the kids were out. Whenever I was at Kathy's, I had to resist the compulsion to tidy up. I hated clutter or untidiness. According to her, I was a little OCD.

"How much sugar?" Kathy asked with a stupid grin on

her face.

Why did we have to play this silly game every time?

"You know how much I take. One and two-third teaspoons."

"One and *two-thirds*?" she mocked. "Are you sure you wouldn't prefer one and *seven-eighths*?"

I ignored her. Can I help it if one and a half isn't enough, but two is too much?

"Biscuit?" Kathy held out the tin.

"No thanks." Why did she insist on putting different kinds of biscuits in the same tin? I had separate Tupperware boxes for each type of biscuit. And no, I don't think that's at all weird.

I managed to negotiate my way back to my seat in the living room without treading on any of the million and one pieces of Lego that were scattered across the floor.

"How much Lego does Lizzie actually have?" I asked, as I sipped the tea. It was a little too sweet. I suspected she'd put two spoonfuls in just to wind me up.

"Too much. Every time we go into town, she pesters me to buy more."

"You should put your foot down."

"That's rich coming from you. Don't you remember what you were like when you were a kid?"

"I didn't have Lego."

"No, but you had enough Beanie Babies to sink a ship."

"I didn't have that many." One hundred and thirty four, to be precise.

"You wouldn't let me go into your bedroom in case I moved one of them."

"That's not true!" It was, but only because Kathy had no idea where each of the beanies was meant to be. She'd take two or three of them off the shelf, and then put them back in the wrong place. It used to drive me insane. "It *is* true," she said. "You had them in alphabetical order."

"I did not." I did — I still do. "Anyway, you were just as bad."

"I didn't have any beanies."

"One word — Barbies."

I'd hated the way that Kathy mistreated her Barbies. She'd strip some of them naked so that she could give their clothes to other dolls. *'They need layers'* she'd say. What about the poor naked Barbies? Some of them had even lost limbs. It was a disgrace.

"I didn't *collect* Barbies," she said.

"You had almost thirty."

"It still wasn't a *collection*. I didn't arrange them in alphabetical order *or* catalogue them. You did!"

"I did not!" I so did. I still had my beanies; they were in the walk-in wardrobe in my flat. Kathy thought I'd got rid of them years ago.

"Anyway, tell me more about this serial killer." Kathy said.

"My client's girlfriend was the latest victim. Her last name was Fox. Apparently, there have been two other murders: Mrs Lyon and Mrs Lamb."

"So, the serial killer is supposedly murdering women who's surname is an animal?"

"Yes, at least according to my client and the Bugle, but not as far as the police are concerned."

"If the Bugle says it's so, it must be." Kathy sneered.

"I know. They've dubbed the killer 'The Animal'."

"Genius."

"The police have dismissed the idea out of hand."

"Why? It must be a possibility. If not, it's one heck of a coincidence."

"The first victim's name was spelled L Y O N not L I O N. According to the police, that means the name connection is just a coincidence."

"What do you think?"

"They're probably right. It seems a little far-fetched that someone would choose his victims based on their surnames. I think my client may be clutching at straws."

"So why did you take the case?"

"I need the money."

"Business that bad?"

"It isn't great. A lot of Dad's regular clients disappeared after he died."

"Why? You're every bit as good as he was. Dad said so himself."

"I don't know. I guess they were just used to dealing with Dad."

I knew I wasn't half the P.I. that Dad had been, but I was no mug either. I'd had a good teacher. Dad had said that I had a natural aptitude for the work.

"Do you think it's because they don't want to do business with a woman?" Kathy said.

"No one has actually come out and said so, but it's a pretty safe bet."

"That's just stupid. Have you got any leads on this case?"

"Not yet. I'm going to start by talking to the husbands of the first two victims to try to get a feel for if there is any connection."

"So?" Kathy had that tone in her voice again. The one she used whenever she was about to nag me—which was most of the time. "How's your love life?"

"Pass." I tried not to think about it—it was way too depressing.

"Are you seeing anyone?"

"Yes." She knew I wasn't.

"Who?"

"No one that you know."

"Are you lying?"

"Yes." I could never fool Kathy—it was pointless even to try. She could read me like a book.

"What about lover boy? That new detective."

"Who?"

"Come on. You know who I mean. Have you spoken to him recently?"

"No."

I'd made the fatal mistake of telling Kathy that I thought a detective, who had recently moved to the area, was pretty hot. What I hadn't known then, but had subsequently discovered, was that he was a total and utter asshat.

"Is he single?" She was relentless as usual.

"How would I know?" I did know—he *was* single. Single and an utter asshat.

"Why don't you ask him out?"

Because I'd rather poke my eye out with a sharp stick—sorry Winky—no offence intended. "I'm not interested. And anyway, I was wrong about him being hot."

"So you don't fancy him?"

"No." I could feel the colour rising in my neck and cheeks. I blushed easily—I always had.

"Why are you blushing then?"

She knew just how to press my buttons. "I don't think he's hot." He was. "I don't fancy him." I did. "There's nothing going on between Detective Maxwell and me." There wasn't.

"Detective Maxwell?" Kathy said. "Why so formal? His name's Jack isn't it? *Jack and Jill.* You two were obviously meant for one another. Come on Jill. Why don't you go up the hill to see Jack?" Kathy broke into her high-pitched squeal of a laugh, just as she did every time she made the same stupid joke.

"Can we please just forget about Jack Maxwell?"

"Okay. I just don't like the idea of you crying *buckets* of tears." She was on a roll now.

"Seriously? Enough of the nursery rhyme jokes." It was time to change the subject. "How's Peter?"

"Pete's Pete. He's fine as always."

Kathy and Peter had been school sweethearts. He'd taken her to the prom, and four years later they'd walked down the aisle together. They were very alike in many ways—except for the baldness obviously. I still couldn't get used to seeing Peter's bald head. At school, he'd had a head of thick, black hair. A few months after they'd married, he started to lose his hair. Within another year, he was almost completely bald, so had started to shave his head. It didn't seem to bother him or Kathy. It did, however, provide me with plenty of ammunition to tease her that she'd been the cause.

"The kids are going to a party this weekend." Kathy picked up a piece of Lego from under one of the chairs. That was her idea of tidying up. "You should come around and have dinner with me and Pete."

"Wouldn't you prefer to spend an evening together—just the two of you?"

"We have plenty of time alone together when the kids are in bed. Besides, I fancy cooking something a little more adventurous than fish fingers. What do you say?"

"Sure. What time?" Unlike me, Kathy was a superb cook, and I was always happy to let someone else do the cooking.

"It'll have to be early because the kids will be back before eight. How about six o'clock?"

"Okay. That'll be nice."

"It most *certainly* will." Kathy grinned, and I immediately realised I'd fallen into a trap.

"Don't you dare try to set me up with someone again."

"Me?" She put on her 'butter wouldn't melt' face, which wasn't fooling anyone—especially not me.

"Kathy! I mean it!"

"What?"

"No more blind dates. Remember what happened last time?"

"How was I supposed to know he picked his nose?"

"And his ears."

"It was just nerves. He'd seemed perfectly fine until then."

"You'd only met him once. At the supermarket!"

"Twice."

"Oh well, that makes all the difference!"

"Okay. I agree it didn't go as well as I'd hoped."

"You think?" His name was Dillon, and I could see why Kathy had noticed him. He was tall, handsome and well spoken. But the man simply couldn't keep his finger out of his nose. It still gave me the creeps just to think about it. "Promise you won't try to set me up again."

"I promise."

I could tell she was lying because her lips were moving.

Chapter 3

It felt good to be back in my own flat. Although I loved Kathy to bits, spending even a few hours at her place drove me insane. I'd no idea how anyone could live with such clutter. Her home wasn't dirty—it was just untidy and disorganised. But then, Kathy's life was disorganised. She'd always been that way. She was never on time, and was always misplacing things.

My flat was on the ground floor; I had a small, private garden at the rear. There was a place for everything, and everything had to be in its place. The flat had a sixties theme. I loved that decade: the music, the clothes and the furniture. I had a vintage record player cabinet on which to play my collection of vinyl records. I had the grooviest little coffee table, which I'd bought from a charity shop— it was an absolute bargain. My two sofas were also sixties style—one yellow and the other orange. Everything in my flat reflected my personality. It was my little oasis of calm.

And Kathy hated it with a passion. She said my furniture reminded her of our late grandma's house. Kathy wouldn't have recognised 'class' if it had punched her on the nose.

My phone rang.

"Jill Gooder."

I listened to the female voice for a few seconds before interrupting. "I'm sorry, but I think you must have the wrong person. My mother died several years ago."

"I'm fairly sure I have the right person," the woman insisted. "The lady who asked me to get in contact with you gave precise instructions. Her name is Darlene Millbright, and she says she's your birth mother."

I felt the colour drain from my face, and had to sit down on the sofa before my legs gave way. When I'd tried to contact my birth mother several years earlier, she'd refused point blank to see me. I hadn't even been able to find out where she lived.

"I—I—err." My brain had disconnected from my mouth.

"I'm sorry to have to tell you this, but your mother is extremely ill. It's unlikely that she'll make it through the night. She really would like to see you before—"

"I'll call you back." I ended the call. I didn't know what else to do. I'd spent so long trying to imagine who my mother might be, what she was like, and of course, why she'd given me up for adoption. At eighteen years of age, I'd tried to track her down, and had been devastated when she'd rejected me again. Perhaps there was still time to get answers to my questions.

I hit the 'Call' button.

"Jill?" Kathy said. "Missing me already?"

"Kathy, listen."

"What's the matter?" Her tone was now serious—she sensed that something was wrong.

"It's my mother. My birth mother."

"What about her?"

"I've had a phone call."

"From her?"

"Yes, well kind of. She's dying. The nursing home called. She wants to see me."

"What are you going to do?"

"I have to go. Will you come with me?"

"Yes, of course. I'll have to arrange for someone to collect the kids from school. Can you pick me up?"

"Could we go in your car? I'm not sure I'm fit to drive." My hands were shaking.

"Sure. I'll be over in twenty minutes."

My heart was racing as I called the nursing home to confirm I was on my way. Why would she ask for me now — now that she was dying? What was I supposed to say to her?

It felt like an eternity until Kathy's green VW pulled up outside my flat.

"Sorry it took me so long." She pushed open the passenger door.

"This doesn't seem real." My head was still spinning as I tried to come to terms with the idea that I might be about to meet my birth mother.

"Where is the nursing home?" Kathy said.

I gave her the piece of paper on which I'd scribbled the address. She studied it for a moment, and then pulled out into traffic without even bothering to indicate. Under normal circumstances, I wouldn't have allowed Kathy to drive me anywhere — she was a maniac on the roads. But these weren't normal circumstances.

"According to this, it's only about five miles away." Kathy glanced at me. "Do you think she might have lived around here all of this time?"

I shrugged. It was too cruel a thought to contemplate. Had she watched me growing up, but never once made contact?

"But I'm her sister," Kathy said.

I thought for a moment she was going to deck the poor nurse.

"I'm very sorry." The nurse stood her ground. "Only Miss Gooder is allowed in."

"This has been a major upset for Jill," Kathy persisted. "She needs someone with her."

"It's okay, Kathy," I said. "I'm fine." I wasn't—I was anything but fine. "Will you wait for me here?"

"Of course. Are you sure you'll be okay?"

I nodded. This was typical of the relationship we'd always had. One moment we were fighting like cat and dog, the next we were in each other's corner.

I followed the nurse along a seemingly never-ending series of corridors. My heart was pounding. I just hoped I wouldn't flake out before I had the chance to meet my mother.

"This is her room." The nurse pushed open the door, and ushered me inside. The bed was surrounded by all manner of drips and monitors. I couldn't bring myself to look at the occupant of the bed. It felt as though my feet were glued to the floor.

"Come closer," a weak voice said. "Jill, come and sit beside me."

I looked up, and for the first time since I was a baby, saw the face of my mother. I'd always had a mental image of what she'd look like. It was an image that had been formed when I was a young child. Back then I'd imagined her to be relatively young—in her thirties or forties maybe. Over the intervening years, I hadn't adjusted that image to take account of the passage of time. The woman I saw looking at me from the bed was nothing like the image I'd carried in my mind for so many years. She looked at least eighty. Her thinning hair was grey; her face was as white as a ghost. It made no sense. How could she be so old? It would have meant she was fifty-plus when she gave birth to me. Perhaps it was her illness that had taken its toll, making her look much older than her years.

"Jill." The woman's eyes were barely open; her voice was little more than a whisper.

"I'm here," I said.

Her thin arm was resting on the top of the bed covers. Her frail fingers opened, and I knew she wanted me to put my hand in hers. I did, and her weak fingers closed around mine.

"Jill," she said again. Her voice seemed to fade with every passing second.

"I'm here." I had so many questions; there was so much I was desperate to know. But it was too late. The woman in front of me was close to death.

"Come closer," she said.

I looked through the window that ran the full length of the room but there was no sign of the nurse. I wished Kathy could have been with me.

"Closer," she said again.

I leaned forward in the chair, stooping so my ear was close to her face. Did she want to tell me something? Perhaps I was going to find out why she'd given me up after all.

"You're a witch!"

The force of her words took me by surprise. From somewhere, she'd mustered the strength to speak much louder than she had previously.

No sooner had she spoken the words, than the monitor changed to one continuous beep. At precisely that moment, something that I can only liken to an electric shock pulsed through my entire body. It was so powerful that it knocked me back into the chair. I felt completely drained. I tried to stand, but my legs didn't want to know.

The door flew open, and a doctor flanked by two nurses rushed to the bedside. It took less than five minutes for him to confirm that my mother had passed away.

"I'm very sorry for your loss," one of the nurses said, after the doctor had left.

"She said I was a—" My words trailed off.

The nurse gave me a sympathetic smile. "Is there anyone we can call?"

"My sister is in the waiting room."

"Are you okay to walk?" The nurse held out her hand.

With her help, I managed to get back to my feet. The walk back felt like a dream.

"Jill!" Kathy rushed over to me. "Are you okay?"

"I want to go home."

"I'm so sorry, Jill." Kathy was driving back to my flat. "Did you get the chance to talk to her at all?"

"Not really. I'd only been with her for a few moments when she died. It was as though she'd been waiting for me."

"And she didn't say anything? Nothing at all?"

My mind went back to my mother's last few moments. And her last words.

"Jill?"

"She said, 'You're a witch'."

"What?"

"She called me a witch." I could feel the tears welling up in my eyes, but I was determined not to cry. I wouldn't allow the woman who had abandoned me to hurt me again.

"Are you sure that's what she said?"

"Oh yes, I'm sure. She used her last ounce of strength to make sure I heard her clearly."

"It doesn't make any sense. Why would she contact you now, just so she could be so unkind?"

"She must have really hated me. It wasn't enough that she'd rejected me. She had to use her dying breath to tell me what she thought of me." I turned to face the side window and wiped away a tear.

"What an evil cow!" Kathy put a hand on my leg. "Don't let it get to you. She isn't worth it. You've been better off without her."

We drove in silence for a while. I could still hear my mother's last words echoing around my head. I wished that she'd never contacted me. I wished that I'd never known who she was or what she thought of me.

"What happens to her now?" Kathy said.

"Sorry?"

"Do you know who is going to organise the funeral?"

"I don't know, and I don't care." Things had happened so quickly that I hadn't thought to ask how my mother had come to be in the nursing home or if she'd had visits from other family members.

Chapter 4

I hadn't expected to sleep well, but as soon as my head hit the pillow, I was out like a light. When I woke the next morning, I felt fitter than I had for months. I'm not usually a morning person, but for some reason I felt as though I could run a marathon. I made a promise to myself that I'd forget all about my birth mother. She'd done more than enough damage. No more.

"Morning, Mrs V."

"Morning, Jill. How are you this beautiful morning?"

"I'm absolutely fantastic. Any mail?"

"Only a few bills. I threw them away."

Mrs V had a system. If the bill wasn't a final demand, she threw it away. It seemed to work. We hadn't been evicted — yet.

"That stupid cat won't drink his milk." She took out her latest knitting project from the bottom drawer of her desk. Needless to say, it was a scarf.

"Did you give him full cream?"

"They didn't have any. I had to get semi-skimmed."

Winky would only drink full cream milk. He turned his nose up at anything else. Mrs V knew that, but refused to pander to him.

"Okay. I'll see to him." I walked through to my office; the sound of knitting needles echoed behind me.

"Meow!" Winky jumped onto my desk, and gave me a one-eyed death stare. "Meow!"

"What's the matter with you?" As if I didn't know. The untouched saucer of milk was under the window. He had to be the most ungrateful cat on the face of the earth.

I'd rescued him from the cats' home when no one else wanted his scary ass, and how did he thank me? By trying to scare off my clients and being precious over what he would and wouldn't drink.

"That old bag knows I only like full cream milk."

"You shouldn't call her that." I stooped down to pick up the saucer. "I'll nip out in a minute to get you some—"

As I spun around to face Winky, I almost spilled the milk. Okay. It was now official. I was going crazy. I thought I'd heard the cat speak, and what was even worse, I'd answered him.

"Meow! Meow!"

"Okay. Okay. I'm going."

"I'm just nipping out for—" I hesitated. "For some biscuits."

Mrs V had started on a new ball of wool. So far, the scarf was red, yellow, green, blue and orange.

"You're going to get full cream milk for that stupid cat, aren't you?" she said, without looking up from her knitting. She knew me too well.

"You know what he's like. He won't drink semi-skimmed."

"Only because you give in to him all the time. He's like a spoiled child."

That was all very well for Mrs V to say. She wasn't the one who had to share an office with the one-eyed feline from hell. If I wanted to get any work done, I'd have to get full cream milk.

"I won't be long."

I bought biscuits—custard creams obviously, a bottle of

over-priced water, which I'd have to hide to avoid Mrs V's *'plenty of water in the tap'* lecture, and a carton of full cream milk.

"There's someone to see you," Mrs V said when I arrived back at the office. She looked accusingly at my bag, making me feel like I was smuggling contraband.

"Who is it?"

"That nice detective."

"Maxwell?" He was many things, but *'nice'* wasn't even on the list.

"That's him. Such a handsome young man."

"Where is he?"

"I sent him through to your office."

"You did what—? Never mind." I'd told Mrs V a thousand times to make sure visitors waited in the outer office, but she had an annoying habit of disregarding my instructions. I wasn't in the mood for Maxwell.

"What's wrong with this cat?" Maxwell had moved his chair away from my desk because Winky was hissing at him.

"He's waiting for this." I opened the carton and poured the milk into the saucer. Winky was off the desk in a flash, and soon purring loudly, as he lapped up the milk.

"I thought he was going to take my eyes out." Maxwell pushed the chair back towards the desk.

I took a seat opposite him. "Nice scarf!"

He tugged at the two-tone green woollen scarf that was wrapped around his neck.

"The lady out front gave it to me."

"That's Mrs V. She likes to knit."

"Don't you mind her knitting when she's supposed to be working?"

"Not really. It's not as though I pay her."

"You don't pay her?" He pulled the scarf a little looser. It looked like a boa constrictor wrapped around his neck. "Taking advantage of the elderly? Not cool."

See what I mean? The man was an asshat. "What's it got to do with you what I pay my staff?"

"You said you *didn't* pay her."

"Why don't you arrest me for slave labour and have done with it?" There was something about the man that set my snark on full throttle.

Mrs V had been with Dad forever. A few months after he died, I'd told her that I couldn't afford to keep her on because business was so quiet. She'd insisted she wanted to continue to work anyway. As far as I knew she had no family, so if she hadn't come into work, she'd have been stuck in the house all alone—all day, every day. Instead, she'd chosen to come into the office—to knit. Scarves— lots of them.

"I don't like to see anyone being taken advantage of," Maxwell said. "Especially not such a sweet old lady."

"Mrs V is more than capable of looking out for herself. She doesn't need you to fight her battles." It hadn't taken long for Maxwell to remind me why I despised him so much. "What can I do for you, Detective?" I was curious as to what had brought him to my office. Although our paths had crossed several times, he'd never been there before.

"I heard you are working on the Caroline Fox case."

"No comment." How exactly had he heard? Did he have my office bugged? Paranoid? Who? Me?

"I don't want you interfering with our investigations."

"Noted." I pictured myself strangling him slowly with

the green scarf.

"I know that Danny Peterson has a bee in his bonnet about a serial killer," he said.

"Apparently, he isn't the only one."

"You mean the Bugle? No one takes that rag seriously, but if you help to fuel this stupid rumour, then the story might get legs. I don't want mass panic over what is no more than silly speculation."

"How can you be so sure that there isn't a serial killer at large?"

"You're going to have to take my word for it."

I wouldn't have taken his word that it was cold, even if there were icicles on the roof.

"Is that everything, Detective?"

"Not quite. Did you know that the first victim's surname was spelled — ?"

"L Y O N. Yes, I did know. That doesn't mean you should discard the serial killer theory. It just means that the murderer can't spell."

"This *isn't* the work of a serial killer."

"You sound awfully sure of that."

"The MOs are different."

"All of them?"

"The first two have similarities, but the third one is completely different."

"How?"

"That's as much as you're getting. I need you to steer clear of this investigation. Tell your client that he's got it wrong, and that he should let us handle it."

"I'm *very* sorry, but I can't do that." I wasn't even the slightest bit sorry.

"It would be better for you if you did."

"Is that some kind of threat? What will you do if I don't leave it alone? Set your scarf on me?"

Maxwell's face reddened. I wasn't sure if he was angry at what I'd said or if the scarf was slowly choking him to death—hopefully the latter.

"I've asked you politely, and now I'm telling you. If there is any interference from you on this investigation, I'll have you arrested for obstructing the police."

I'd had enough of him. I walked across the room and opened the door. "Thank you for dropping in, Detective Maxwell."

He took off the scarf, dropped it onto my desk, and then left without another word.

"Such a nice young man," Mrs V said after he'd left. "Did he ask you out?"

"Not exactly."

"He didn't take his scarf with him."

"He must have forgotten it."

I'd been in such a positive mood, but Maxwell had ruined it.

"This came for you while you were with the detective." Mrs V handed me an envelope marked 'Special Delivery.'

Back in my office, I found Winky curled up in the scarf that Maxwell had dropped onto the desk. I closed the door quickly so Mrs V wouldn't see him—she'd have had a fit.

The postmark on the envelope was indecipherable. The letter inside had been beautifully hand-written. It was signed 'Aunt Lucy,' and was apparently from my birth mother's sister. It explained that my mother had insisted on moving to the nursing home only a week before her death. She'd done it with the intention of contacting me. Apparently, I had more family: two cousins, a grandmother, and of course the writer of the letter. She said that the main reason for writing was to invite me to attend my mother's funeral, which was to be held in a village called Candlefield in two days time. On the back of the letter was a hand-drawn map with directions to Candlefield, which was apparently twenty miles away. Strange, I'd never even heard of the place.

The sudden appearance of my birth mother had tilted my world. Learning that I had a whole new family was threatening to knock it off its axis. Since my adopted parents had died, the only family I'd had were Kathy, Peter and the kids. Now, suddenly, I had an aunt, a grandma and two cousins. And, I'd been invited to attend my mother's funeral.

"How's tricks?" Peter, my brother-in-law, greeted me at the door.

"Okay, thanks." I forced a smile. I hadn't felt like going out, but Kathy had persuaded me it would take my mind off things. I was a little apprehensive in case she'd decided to set me up on another blind date. What could I expect this time? A guy who cut his toenails at the dinner table? I peered around the living room door.

"It's okay," Kathy said. "I haven't invited anyone else. I was going to, but after the last few days, I thought you might be feeling a little fragile."

"Your sister is more than capable of finding herself a man," Peter said.

"Thank you, Peter." I wished I shared his confidence.

"No she isn't," Kathy said. "Look at all the losers she's

been with."

"Thanks, sis!"

"It's true. Look at your track record."

She was right, but I could have done without the reminder. "At least the guys I found for myself didn't pick their noses."

"You should date Jack Maxwell," Kathy said.

"Who's he?" Peter asked.

"Jill's new detective friend. He's hot!"

"He is *not* my friend."

"He is hot though. You said so yourself."

"I didn't."

"You so did. You gushed about him."

"I've never *gushed* in my life."

"You told me he was *panty-melting* hot!"

Sometimes I hated my sister. Usually when she was right. "I never said that!"

"Whatever." Kathy sighed. "What did he do to upset you this time?"

"He tried to warn me off the Fox murder case."

"The serial killer?"

"What serial killer?" Peter's ears pricked up.

"There is no serial killer." I was regretting telling Kathy already.

"There might be. You said so yourself."

"Anyway. Maxwell said if I continued with my investigation that he'd charge me with obstruction."

"Does that mean you're off the case?"

"What do you think?" Jack Maxwell's visit had made me even more determined to stay involved with the Fox case. I liked nothing better than solving the police's cases for them.

"You need to be careful," Kathy said. "Dad tried to avoid conflict with the police. Do you remember what he used to say? Softly, softly catchee tiger."

"Monkey."

"What?"

"It's 'softly, softly, catchee monkey'."

"Whatever. I'm only trying to help." Kathy sighed. "I can handle the police. Now can we please forget about Jack Maxwell?"

"I still think you should date him." Kathy always had to have the last word.

"Not happening." So did I.

"Thanks. That was great." I'd just eaten the last spoonful of sticky, toffee pudding. "You must let me do the washing up."

"Sit down!" Peter said, already on his feet. "I'll do it while you two gossip."

"I do not gossip!" Kathy protested.

"Yes, you do!" I said. "It's what you do best."

Peter disappeared into the kitchen and shut the door behind him. I wasn't sure if that was to give us privacy, or so that he didn't have to listen to our jabbering.

"Haven't you noticed anything?" Kathy held out her arms expansively.

Had she bought new furniture? It couldn't be that—I'd have already noticed. She hadn't changed her hair. I shrugged.

"The room. It's tidy. I spent all afternoon tidying up."

"Oh yeah. Of course." Kathy's idea of tidy and mine were miles apart. I'd noticed Lego pieces under the armchair while I was eating dinner. And the ornaments on the mantelpiece were facing the wrong way. "It looks great!"

Kathy seemed pleased. "It won't stay this way for long. As soon as the kids are back, it'll be like a bomb-site again."

"I've had a letter from my birth mother's sister," I said. I'd been debating all evening whether or not to tell Kathy.

"You have more family?"

"So it would seem. An aunt, a grandma and two cousins."

"Wow! How do you feel about that?"

"I don't know. I'm still in shock."

"What did the letter say? Did you bring it with you?"

"No. It was actually an invitation to the funeral."

"Will you go?"

"I'm not sure. I doubt it. Not after what she said to me on her death bed."

"She was probably delirious. It could have been the drugs. She might not have known what she was saying."

"Maybe." I didn't believe that for a second. My mother had put so much effort into getting out those last words. She'd known exactly what she was saying.

"I could go with you if you want."

"No. It's okay. If I do go, I'd rather go by myself." I didn't want to tell Kathy that the invitation had specifically said I must attend alone.

Chapter 5

It was raining on the day of the funeral. I'd wrestled with my decision ever since the letter arrived. A part of me had wanted to forget all about my birth mother. After the way she'd treated me, why should I waste another second thinking about her? In the end, I decided that I'd never forgive myself if I didn't attend her funeral. Even though she'd rejected me more than once, I still owed my very existence to the woman who had used her dying breath to insult me. The other factor in my decision had been the opportunity to meet my 'other' family. Perhaps they'd be able to throw some light on why my mother had given me up for adoption, why she'd refused to see me when I tried to contact her, and why she'd asked to see me from her death-bed.

I hardly slept the night before. By six o' clock, I couldn't see the point in lying in bed a minute longer. I had to force myself to eat breakfast. I was so nervous I actually felt as though I might be sick.

Kathy phoned me a little after seven. "Are you okay?" She sounded sleepy, and I could hear the kids shouting in the background. "I wasn't sure if you'd be up."

"I've been up since six. Couldn't sleep."

"Are you still planning to go?"

"Yeah. I think so, unless I lose my nerve between now and then."

"I wish you'd let me come with you. I don't like to think of you doing this alone."

"I'll be okay, honestly. I'd rather go alone." The truth was I'd have given anything to have Kathy go with me. What was with my crazy, new family? Who dictates who can and can't attend a funeral?

"If you change your mind, give me a call."

"I'll be fine. I promise."

After four miles, I began to have doubts as to whether or not I was headed in the right direction. I'd expected to see a signpost for Candlefield a mile back. I did a quick U-turn and drove back the way I'd come. There was still no signpost. I was working from memory because I'd left the directions on the kitchen worktop. Maybe I was on the wrong road altogether.

I pulled into a lay-by and typed Candlefield into the SatNav. The response said '*Unknown - try again*'. I tried every combination of spelling that I could think of, but they all drew a blank. It made no sense. I had no choice but to head back to my flat to get the letter.

I rushed in, grabbed it and rushed out again. The directions were very straightforward, and it seemed that I'd been on the right road, so why hadn't I seen the sign? I retraced my original route, and after three miles saw the signpost for Candlefield. How had I missed it twice before? My mind must have been even more scrambled than I'd thought.

I checked the time — I was running almost thirty minutes late. What a way to make a great first impression. What would my new family think of me? Did I care?

Yes.

I'd lived in Washbridge all of my life, and I'd travelled around the surrounding area extensively. So how come I'd never heard of Candlefield? Since taking the turn at the signpost, I hadn't recognised any of the roads I'd driven along. I promised myself that when I had more time, I'd come back and explore the area more thoroughly.

Twenty minutes later, I saw the sign 'Welcome to Candlefield'. The approach to the village was across a narrow bridge that was only wide enough for a single vehicle. Once over the bridge, the road wound its way up a hill. Quaint cottages, some of them thatched, bordered the road on either side. Candlefield was beautiful. There were very few people on the streets. Since crossing the bridge, I'd seen one elderly man, a young man on a bike, and a young woman with two children.

The church was perched on top of the hill. I was almost thirty minutes late. Maybe it would be best if I simply turned around and drove home. It seemed disrespectful to turn up so late. The rain, which had been little more than drizzle when I'd set off, was now much heavier. As I climbed out of the car, I could see a crowd of mourners in the distance. That had to be them.

"Great!" I'd left my umbrella back at the flat. This day was just getting better and better. I made my way through the gates, and began to walk towards the crowd of mourners. By the time I reached them, I would look like a drowned rat.

"Step under this."

I almost jumped out of my skin. I hadn't seen the woman approach me. She was dressed in black, and was holding a large umbrella.

"Thanks." I dipped under it. "I didn't see you there."

"You must be Jill." The woman smiled.

I nodded.

"I'm your aunt Lucy. We hoped you would come, but we were beginning to think you weren't going to make it."

"I'm really sorry. The SatNav couldn't find Candlefield. I had to go back for the map you sent me." The excuse sounded lame even to me.

"Not to worry. You're here now, and that's all that matters. Your mother would have been so happy to know you came."

"What about my father? Is he still — ?"

Aunt Lucy shook her head.

I glanced ahead and could see the mourners were beginning to disperse. The majority of them were taking another path that led to a second set of gates to my right.

"We're going back to my house," she said. "You're welcome to come. I know the rest of the family would love to meet you."

"I — I don't think I'm ready for that. Not yet."

"Not to worry. There will be plenty of time for you to meet them another day. Now you know where we are, you're welcome to visit at any time."

We walked in silence to the now deserted graveside. I stared down at the coffin.

"She loved you more than anything in the world," Aunt Lucy said.

"How can you say that?" The words were out before I had the chance to filter them. "Sorry. I didn't mean to — "

"It's okay." She smiled. "This must be difficult for you."

More difficult than she could know. I wanted to run back to the car, drive home, and forget I'd ever heard from my mother. But first I needed answers.

"Why did she reject me?"

"She didn't." Aunt Lucy put her hand on my shoulder. "You must never think that."

"What am I supposed to think? She put me up for adoption when I was a baby, and then refused to see me when I tried to find her."

"That broke your mother's heart."

"Then why do it?"

"It's complicated."

"Not from where I'm standing." I tried to control my emotions, but my anger forced its way to the surface. "Do you know what her last words to me were?"

Aunt Lucy shook her head.

"She called me a witch! A witch! If she loved me, why would she do that? She could have used her last breath to tell me why she had to give me up for adoption, or at least to tell me she loved me. If she'd done that, maybe I could have forgiven her, but not now."

I pulled away. Aunt Lucy tried to grab my hand, but I hurried back along the path to my car. I don't remember the journey back. I must have been on auto-pilot.

Rather than go straight home, I called at Kathy's. She looked surprised to see me.

"Did you change your mind?"

"What about?"

"The funeral. No one will blame you." She gave me a peck on the cheek. "Come on in, I was about to make a cup of tea."

As I walked through to the living room, I noticed the clock on the wall. Ten o' clock. The funeral had been at nine-thirty. I hadn't arrived in Candlefield until almost ten because I'd got lost. How could it be ten o' clock?

"Are you okay?" Kathy looked concerned.

"Yeah. I'm fine." Apart from losing my mind.

"Don't beat yourself up about it. No one will think any worse of you for not going. Not after the way she treated you."

"I did go."

"Oh? I thought you said it was at nine-thirty? Here, drink this." She passed me the tea. "Did you meet your new family?"

"Only my aunt Lucy. She kept trying to tell me how much my mother had loved me. Yeah, right."

"What about your father?"

"Dead."

"Oh, Jill. I'm so sorry."

"It's okay. It's not like I ever knew him."

"What about your cousins and grandma? What were they like?"

"I didn't get to meet them. I arrived late. By the time I got there, the ceremony was over. Aunt Lucy did invite me back to her place, but I couldn't face it. I had to get away."

"Maybe you could go back there when you're feeling up to it."

"I'm never going back there."

"But they're your family."

"You're my only family. I've managed without them this long. I can manage without them now."

"What about the village? What's it like?"

"Beautiful. Picture postcard beautiful. I can't believe I've never even heard of it before."

Kathy pulled out her phone and fired up Google Maps. "What did you say it was called?"

"Candlefield."

"How are you spelling that?"

"Candle and then field. One word."

"That's what I thought. Google doesn't recognise it. Are you sure you've got the name right?"

"Positive."

"Well it isn't on here."

"I had the same problem with the SatNav. Very weird. When we have some free time, I'll take you there. It's really gorgeous."

"Why don't you stay with us for a few days? I don't like to think of you all alone after what you've been through."

I didn't take her up on the offer. Much as I loved my nephew and niece, I needed my own space and a little peace and quiet. I wouldn't get either at Kathy's. Once I was back at my flat, I tried to distract myself with a little TV, but I couldn't focus. My mind refused to be still; it kept returning to the events of the day. Perhaps I should have gone to the wake. But why? I was an outsider; I wasn't *really* family.

I needed something to occupy my mind, and I remembered something Mrs V had said some months earlier: '*There's nothing quite like it to relax the mind*'. She'd been trying to persuade me to take up knitting. I'd pooh-poohed the idea at the time, and certainly hadn't given her any reason to believe I was interested. That hadn't stopped her from buying me a 'starter kit', which comprised of two balls of wool, a pair of knitting needles and a 'beginner's guide'. Ever since then, she'd asked me at least once a week how I was getting on with it.

Depending on how I felt, I'd either tell her I'd been too busy or I'd lie and say *'it's coming along'*. In truth I hadn't looked at it since the day she'd given it to me when I'd thrown it — now where had I thrown it?

Twenty minutes later, I found it at the bottom of the wardrobe. Unsurprisingly, the pattern that came with the beginner's guide was for a scarf. How difficult could it be?

Are you kidding me? How could there be only forty-five stitches — there should be forty-six. It just wasn't possible. I'd taken it really slowly this time. It was my fourth attempt, and so far I'd lost stitches every single time. Where did they go? Was there a 'knitting fairy' that magicked them away when I wasn't looking? No wonder Mrs V was border-line crazy. This knitting lark was enough to send anyone bonkers.

Two hours and no scarf later, I gathered up the wool, needles and beginners guide, and threw them back into the wardrobe. Next time I needed to soothe my nerves, I'd hit the vodka.

Chapter 6

My usual breakfast comprised a cup of tea and cereal. The morning after the funeral, I had two strong cups of coffee. I needed them just to get me out of the door. The events of the previous day had left me exhausted.

"Morning, Mrs V."
"Morning, dear. Are you okay? You look a little tired this morning."
"I didn't sleep very well. I have a few things on my mind right now."
Mrs V looked over her half-moon glasses. "I know just the thing for that."
Don't you dare—just don't you—
"Knitting. It's what has kept me sane all of these years. Do you still have the—?"
I went through to my office and slammed the door closed behind me. I could hear Mrs V tutting through the glass. One of the reasons I felt so tired was because I'd had a nightmare in which I'd been searching high and low for dropped stitches.
"Meow!" Winky rubbed against my legs. "Meow!"
I stroked his head, "Here's a tip for you, boy. Don't ever take up knitting."
I walked over to the window, and hung my coat on the stand. When I turned around I found Winky sitting on my chair. "Off you get!" I tapped his backside, and he jumped down. "You've got plenty of seats to choose from. You can't have mine."
I stooped down to get the 'Caroline Fox' folder out of the filing cabinet.

"Your chair is the most comfortable."
I banged my head as I shot back up.
"Meow! Meow!"
I stared at him. He stared back—as best he could. Okay,
now I was hearing things. I truly was losing my mind.

Normally, once I'm on a case, I'm laser-focussed, but I'd
really dropped the ball this time. With all the upheaval
of the previous few days, I'd barely thought about the
'Fox' case since Danny Peterson's visit. Billable hours to-
date came to precisely zero. That wouldn't pay the rent
or keep Winky in full cream milk. I did a quick read
through of my notes to get back up to speed. I really was
beginning to have second thoughts on whether or not I
should have taken the case, but it was too late to back
out now. I'd made a promise to Danny, and the least I
could do was dig around and see what I could come up
with. I couldn't contact Mr Lyon, so decided to start with
Mr Lamb, husband of the second murder victim. It
wasn't difficult to find his phone number and address.
By midday, it was obvious that he had no intention of
answering his phone or responding to the numerous
messages I'd left for him. That left me with only one
option.
Just my luck. There was nowhere to park within sight of
the house, so I had to leave my car several streets away.
Trust me to pick the coldest day of the year so far. I
managed to find a little shelter from the icy cold wind by
leaning against a tree that was on the opposite side of the
road to Lamb's house. I'd already tried knocking on his
door, and I'd stolen a look through the front window,
but there was no sign of life. I'd also checked the garage,

but his car wasn't there. My plan was to doorstep him when he got back. That was if I didn't die from hypothermia first.

It was a nice, quiet neighbourhood. Not the type of place you'd expect to find a murderer—serial killer or otherwise. I noticed an elderly woman staring at me from an upstairs window in the house behind me. She was probably Neighbourhood Watch. Hopefully Mr Lamb would return home before I was hauled away by the police.

"Mr Lamb?" I chased after him as soon as he got out of the car.

"I have nothing to say." He was nothing like I'd expected him to be. For some reason I'd pictured a mild-mannered, accountant type. Instead what I got was a real bruiser who could have passed for a serial killer quite easily. Bald, apart from tufts of hair on either side of his head, he stood about five-eight tall. He was a little overweight, but not what you would call fat. He looked like he hadn't had a shave for at least a week.

"Go away!" he snarled.

"I just want a few words." I was already back-pedalling.

"I'm not talking to the press!"

"I'm not the press."

"Course you aren't. That's what they all say."

"It's true." I slid my hand into my inside pocket and pulled out a card. "Look."

He glanced at the card. "P.I? You don't look like a P.I."

Which when translated meant 'you're not a man'.

"My name's Jill Gooder. I've called several times today and left messages."

"I don't listen to my messages any more."

"Right. Of course. I understand. Look, I'm working for Danny Peterson."

"Who? Never heard of him."

"He's the boyfriend of Caroline Fox." The name seemed to register with Lamb. "She was murdered a few days ago. He thinks her murder might be connected to your wife's."

"Because of her name? The police told me the Bugle article about a serial killer was nonsense."

"Maybe. Maybe not. That's what I want to find out."

Mr Lamb's demeanour had softened — enough for me to feel comfortable taking a few steps towards him. "Could we go inside to talk about this?" My nose and ears were freezing.

He looked back at the house, and then at me again. "Okay. Come in. But if I find out you're press—"

Once we were inside, Mr Lamb dropped the aggression, and even offered me a coffee.

"Biscuit?"

I hesitated. I didn't want to appear rude, but the biscuits were all mixed together. I had to suppress a shudder. "No, thanks. Got to think of my figure."

"You women. My wife was always on a diet." He picked up a framed photo, and handed it to me. The woman was beautiful, and certainly had no need of a diet.

"That was taken last Christmas."

I could hear the hurt in his voice.

"She was beautiful," I said.

"Much too beautiful for an ugly brute like me."

"I'm sure that's not true." It definitely was. Mr Lamb

had been punching well above his weight.

"It is true. She was much too good for me in every way. I couldn't believe my luck when she said she'd go out with me. When she agreed to be my wife, I couldn't have been any happier."

I smiled. Words seemed inadequate.

"Then someone stole her away from me. If I ever lay my hands on him, he'll wish that he was dead."

"Have the police said if they have any leads?"

"They seem clueless. Every time I ask what's happening, they say that they're 'pursuing a number of lines of enquiry.' What does that mean? It's all double-talk. I'd been thinking about doing the same thing—contacting a P.I., but I didn't know where to begin. Are you any good?"

"You'd have to ask my clients, but yes, I like to think so. My father was a P.I."

"Family business eh? That's nice. Maybe you could work for me too?"

"If it turns out the cases are connected, then I guess I will be doing—in a manner of speaking. Is it okay if I ask you a few questions?"

He nodded.

"What can you tell me about the day your wife was murdered?"

"It was just a normal day. Trisha had been to the book club at the library—she went there every Wednesday afternoon. She loved to read. Not me—I'm more of a TV kind of guy. Most nights, if we weren't going out, I'd watch TV while Trisha read her books. She liked Romance novels. I offered to watch TV upstairs, so as not to disturb her, but she said that once she was engrossed in a good book, all other sounds faded into the background."

"What about the days leading up to her death? Anything out of the ordinary? Anything at all?"

"Nothing. We lived a fairly routine kind of life. Boring, you might say. Trisha did the weekly shop, went to the gym, and visited her brother."

"Do you have a contact number for him?"

"It's on my phone." He flicked through his list of contacts until he had it. "There you go."

We talked for over an hour. Most of that time, I spent listening to Mr Lamb reminisce about the woman who had been the love of his life. His soul mate.

As I left, I promised to keep him posted on events. He offered to pay me, but I declined. I didn't feel right about taking two payments for the same case. I was pleased to have made contact with Mr Lamb, but I didn't feel that I'd learned anything new. From what he'd told me, there was no obvious reason why anyone would have wanted to kill his wife. The more I thought about it, the more it felt like a senseless, random attack, which was precisely how the police were treating it from all accounts.

On the drive home, I felt my phone vibrate. I ignored it until I arrived back at my flat. There was a voice mail from Jack Maxwell: *'I told you to stay away from the Fox case, and yet you paid a visit to Mr Lamb today. I won't tell you again. Stay out of police business. All you are doing is hindering our enquiries.'*

Who did he think he was? I pressed 'delete'.

Even though it was only four o'clock, I decided to call it

a day. I was feeling pretty frazzled, and there had to be a few perks to being your own boss. I called Mrs V to make sure there was nothing that needed my attention.

"Only that damn cat. He's driving me insane."

I didn't ask why. Mrs V and Winky would have to sort out their differences by themselves for once.

Back at my flat, I decided what I needed was a lazy, self-indulgent evening. That meant a hot bath, followed by a takeaway pizza, a glass of wine, and an enormous bar of chocolate. Just what the doctor ordered.

Before I had a chance to put my plan into action, there was a knock on the door. Much as I loved Kathy, I prayed it wouldn't be her. I just wanted some '*me, myself, I*' time.

"Jill Gooder?" The badge on the young man's jacket read 'Lightning Couriers'. His hair certainly looked as though he'd been struck by lightning.

"That's me."

"Sign here." He passed me one of those ridiculous, hand-held thingamajigs and a plastic stick.

"Where?"

"Anywhere on the screen. Don't matter."

"I can't see what I'm writing."

"Don't worry. Just scribble something."

I scribbled 'Winky the cat' — not that I could read it, and then took the package from him. Although it was only about twelve inches square, it weighed a ton. There was no card or anything else that might have indicated who'd sent it.

I tore off the wrapping to reveal a black box. The lid was fastened down with tape on each side. I grabbed a pair of scissors from the kitchen, and sliced each piece of tape in turn. Inside was a leather-bound book, which looked as though it was a thousand years old. On the front, in large gold letters, the title read 'Spells'.

Was this some kind of joke? What else could it be? Not satisfied with calling me a witch with her dying breath, my mother must have arranged to have this delivered to me after her death. She really had been a piece of work. I was beginning to realise how lucky I'd been to grow up without her.

I lifted the book out of the box, laid it on the coffee table, and opened the front cover. My mother must have gone to a lot of trouble and expense to do this. I hoped it had made her happy. What a sicko!

Chapter 7

I began to flick through the pages. As far as I could tell the 'spells' appeared in no particular order. They certainly weren't listed alphabetically and there was no obvious theme.

Just for a laugh, I decided to read a few of them. I started with 'perfect cakes'. According to the description, it did pretty much 'what it said on the label' — it created perfect cupcakes. It was a pity that it was nonsense because, as the world's worst baker, I could have done with some help on the cake front.

It seemed to me that whoever had come up with the 'Spell' book really hadn't done their research. Everyone knew that spells required things like the wing of bat or the wart of toad. These spells didn't have anything like that. Instead, the instructions required only that I process a sequence of mental images. For example, 'perfect cakes' required me to picture: a golden beach, a waterfall, a blackbird and a ladybird. It all sounded rather 'hippy' and total nonsense.

My phone rang — unknown number, but I recognised the voice immediately.

"Jill? It's Aunt Lucy."

"Oh? Hi." How had she come by my phone number?

"I hope you don't mind me calling you?"

"Err. No. That's okay."

"I'm sorry you had to rush off the other day. I guess all of this must have come as a shock to you?"

No kidding. "Yes, it has."

"The rest of the family were disappointed they didn't get the chance to meet you. We'd all love for you to come over again once you're feeling up to it."

Not a chance. "I'll have to see."

"Of course, my dear. There's no rush. We'll still be here when you've had time to let it all sink in."

"Okay. Thanks. Bye then—"

"Jill! Wait! That's not why I called."

"Why *did* you call?" My impatience was beginning to show, but I didn't really care.

"I wanted to check you'd received the book."

"You sent it?"

"Yes. Your mother asked me to send it to you—in the event of her death. Normally, you'd have started learning spells when you were a child, but—"

"But I wasn't there." I spat the words. "My mother had given me away."

"Jill, I told you. It wasn't like that. Your mother truly—"

"Stop! Please don't try to tell me that she loved me. A mother who loves her child does not use her dying breath to call her a witch."

"Jill! Please! It wasn't like that, I promise. It was—"

"Complicated. I know. You've already said. Well, it isn't complicated now. In fact, it's very straight forward. I want nothing more to do with you or the rest of my so-called family."

"If we could just meet, I could explain."

"Sorry, but no. Please don't contact me again."

"Jill! The book—"

"I'm going to burn it." I ended the call. My hands were shaking.

My phone rang again. What was the matter with that woman? Why wouldn't she take the hint?

"I don't want to speak to you—" I yelled down the phone.

"Wow!" Kathy said. "What did I do?"

"Kathy?" I'd been so wound up that I hadn't even checked the caller ID. "Sorry. I didn't realise it was you." I plonked myself down on the sofa. The stupid book was still open on the coffee table—taunting me.

"Are you okay?" Kathy sounded concerned. She obviously thought I'd finally lost it.

"Yeah. Sorry about that."

"Who did you think I was?"

"Aunt Lucy."

"What on earth did she do to make you so angry? It sounded like you wanted to kill her."

"It doesn't matter."

"Tell me."

"She sent me a book. It— I—"

"What kind of book?"

"Do you remember I told you what my mother said on her death-bed?"

"When she called you a witch?"

"Yeah. Well it seems that she must have had the whole thing planned."

"Had what planned? You aren't making any sense."

"She had Aunt Lucy send me a book on magic spells."

Kathy laughed.

"It isn't funny!"

"It is a bit. Come on, Jill. Your new family are obviously as nutty as fruit cakes. What does the book look like?"

"It's big. Old—Wait! What does it matter what the book looks like?"

"Sorry. Look, I'll come round."

"No, it's okay."

"I'm coming. I'll be there in twenty."

So much for my quiet, relaxing evening. I knew what Kathy was like. She'd insist on trying the stupid spells. I had to get rid of the book before she arrived or she'd be here until the early hours of the morning.

I took it to the communal skip, which was behind the shops. It hit the bottom of the skip with a satisfying thud. Good riddance.

While I was there, I decided to buy a packet of custard creams because I knew Kathy would make short work of the few I had left in the flat. It was always the same. She'd say *'I'll just have one'* and then proceed to scoff the lot.

As I came out of the shop, my heart sank. Mr Ivers, a man who could bore for England, was headed my way. It was too late to duck back inside because he'd already seen me. He lived alone and was an avid cinema-goer. It was the only thing he ever talked about. I couldn't remember the last time I'd been to the cinema. I watched the occasional movie online, but that was about it. Whenever I bumped into him, he insisted on telling me all about the movies he'd watched recently. And he watched an awful lot of them. Apparently he paid a monthly subscription, which meant he could watch as many as he liked. I'd become good at avoiding him, but today I was cornered.

"Oh, hello there." He beamed. "I haven't seen you for a while."

"I've been rather busy."

I tried to side-step him, but he mirrored my move.

"Have you seen any good movies recently?" he asked.

"Like I said before, I don't often go to the cinema."

"You really should. There have been some real blockbusters recently. Last weekend, I went to see Morgan's Secret. You must have read about it. It stars—"

"Sorry, that's my sister. I'll have to go." Kathy's car had just pulled up outside my flat.

"Oh? Okay. Maybe I—"

I didn't hang around to hear what else he had to say.

"Kathy!" I shouted.

"Are you okay?" She took the bag of shopping from me. "You bought custard creams. Great, I'm starving." She led the way inside. "I can't wait to see this book."

As soon as I stepped into the living room, I saw it. Right there on the coffee table—the book of spells.

But how? Someone must have taken it out of the skip while I was in the shop. But who? Was Aunt Lucy stalking me? And if so, how had she got inside the flat?

Kathy walked through to the kitchen, put the shopping on the worktop, and then came back into the living room. "So? Where's this mysterious book?"

"It—it's there." I pointed.

"This?" Now it was Kathy's turn to look puzzled as she stared at the book.

"Yes."

"This little thing?" She leaned forward and put her hand on the front cover. "I thought you said it was some kind of magic book?"

I did a double-take. Kathy was flicking through a small hardback book titled 'Magical cooking in 5 days'.

I snatched the book away from her. The thin, modern-looking volume weighed almost nothing.

"Jill? Are you sure you're okay?"

"This isn't the book. It's changed."

"Changed?"

"It shouldn't even be here. I threw it in the skip."

"Are there two books?"

"No. Yes. I don't know."

Kathy took the book from me and placed it back on the coffee table. "I think you need to lie down." She put her hand on my shoulder. "This thing with your mother has affected you more than you're admitting."

"I'm okay." Was I though? I was beginning to have doubts.

Kathy led me through to the bedroom, and insisted I lay on the bed. I was too dazed to argue. What had happened? I'd thrown the book in the skip, but it had somehow come back. Or had it? Now it was a different book. Or were there two books? Maybe things would make more sense if I had a drink. "I need vodka."

"I don't think that would be a good idea. I'll make you a cup of tea."

"Pour me a vodka."

"You're having tea, and that's an end to it."

See? I told you she was bossy.

"Here." She passed me the cup of tea. "Do you want a biscuit?" she said through a mouthful of custard creams. "Are there any left?"

"I've only had two—or three—maybe four, but definitely not more than five. And, I've hidden the vodka."

"Thanks." Little did she know I had another bottle under the sink.

"Both bottles."

Bum!

"Maybe I should stay with you tonight," Kathy said, eyeing up the packet of biscuits.

"Why? So you can finish off the custard creams?"

"I'm worried about you. You've been acting a bit weird. I could ring Pete."

"No! I'll be okay. I promise."

"It's no bother."

"Honestly. I'll be fine."

It took me a while, but I eventually persuaded her that I was well enough to be left alone. Someone was playing tricks on me, and I wasn't impressed. I stayed in the bedroom for a few minutes after she left just in case she doubled back to check on me — she could be sneaky like that. I hardly dared look at the coffee table, for fear of what I might see. The book was right there — not the cute little baking book that Kathy had seen, but the book of spells. The one I'd thrown into the skip.

Okay, I needed to recap. I'd put the book in the skip. When I'd returned to the flat, the book was on the coffee table. It had then transformed into the baking book. And then it had transformed back into the book of spells. Confused? I certainly was, but somehow I had to find a logical explanation.

Someone could have taken the book out of the skip and brought it back to my flat while I was in the shop, but how had they got in? There was no sign of forced entry. Could I have left the door unlocked? No, because I'd had to unlock it when I came back with Kathy. How had the book changed from an old book of spells into a modern, lightweight book on baking? There must have been two books, and someone must have swapped them.

The only explanation that made even a lick of sense was that someone must have got into the flat, and they must still have been there when Kathy and I returned. But how come I hadn't seen them make the switch? Could whoever it was still be in the flat?

I went into my bedroom, and picked up Dad's old golf club, which I always kept under the bed. The flat wasn't very big, and there were a limited number of places that anyone could hide. I checked the bathroom and then the spare bedroom. Then I checked all the large cupboards and the walk-in wardrobe. Finally, I had a quick look around the garden. All clear, but I was still convinced that someone must have been in the flat while I was in the shop.

I found the number of a local locksmith and gave him a call. He said he could be with me within three hours. I considered taking the book back to the skip, but I didn't really want to leave the flat again until the locks had been changed. As soon as they had, I'd get rid of the stupid book once and for all.

Chapter 8

This was the final straw. Kathy knew how much I hated different types of biscuit being mixed together, and yet she'd put the remaining custard creams in with the digestives. There was no way I could eat them now. The only other biscuits I had in the flat were ginger-nuts, which are nice enough, but not when you had your heart set on a custard cream. The shops would probably be closed by the time the locksmith had been. Great! Thanks, Kathy!

What was that?
I thought I'd heard a noise coming from my bedroom. I didn't see how anyone could be in there because I'd searched every nook and cranny. Still, I wasn't about to take any chances, so I walked on tip-toe over to the bedroom door, turned the handle as slowly and quietly as I could, and stepped inside.
There was no-one in there.

Time was dragging. I wished the locksmith would hurry up so I could relax and enjoy what was left of the evening. I flicked through the pages of the book of spells while I waited. Who'd written this thing? Obviously, someone with more time than sense.
I spotted a spell titled 'invisible'. It was one of the shorter ones. According to the crazy book, it gave you ten minutes of invisibility—yeah—of course it did. This was obviously some kind of wind up to see if anyone was gullible enough to actually try it. There was even a warning that after the invisibility had worn off you had

to wait another thirty minutes before you could repeat the spell.

Okay, why not? It's not like I had anything else to do while I was waiting. I began to follow the instructions, picturing the images one by one: a rainbow, a white feather, an eagle, a lion, and so on.

Thank goodness there was no one around to see me making such a fool of myself. When I'd finished, and even though I knew it was totally bonkers, I glanced down—just in case I'd turned invisible. Well, what a surprise. There I was—not invisible at all.

The knock on the door made me jump. I slammed the book closed, and slid it under the sofa. I didn't want the locksmith to think he was dealing with a nutter.

He was middle-aged with a round face and ruddy cheeks. A big man, he looked as though he enjoyed his food. The logo on his overalls was of a robin holding a key. The name of the company was, unsurprisingly, Robin Security.

"Hello?" he shouted straight at my face.

"Hello," I said.

"Hello?" he shouted again.

What was wrong with this guy?

"Hi," I said, and waved my hand in front of his face.

"Anyone in?" He started forward, so I took a step to the side.

A joke was a joke, but this had gone far enough. "Excuse me," I said, in my sternest voice. "Do you mind?"

"Hello? Anyone home?" He peered into the kitchen, and then turned back to the living room. He was staring straight at me, as he wiped a hand across his brow. He looked almost as confused as I was. If I didn't know better I'd have said this was one of Kathy's wind-ups, but she didn't even know I'd called the locksmith.

The front door was still open, and I heard footsteps in the corridor. I stepped out just in time to see the last person on earth I needed right now. Mr Ivers was headed straight towards me. I was already running through my list of excuses when he walked straight past me without a word — without even a glance. That now familiar cold sensation began to run through my veins. It wasn't possible. I knew it wasn't possible. And yet, apparently, neither the locksmith nor Mr Ivers could see me. There had to be an explanation, and preferably one that hadn't just arrived on the crazy town bus.

The locksmith had apparently given up trying to find me, and had taken a seat on one of the sofas. He checked his watch, and tutted to himself. What was I supposed to do now? As I made my way past him, he never even flinched.

I stood in front of the full length mirror in the bedroom. All I could see was a reflection of the room behind me. It seemed that if I looked directly at myself, I was visible, but to other people, or in a mirror, I was invisible. But I couldn't be invisible — that was impossible! There had to be some other explanation. Maybe none of this was real. Maybe Kathy had slipped something into my cup of tea and I was hallucinating. Maybe I was running out of maybes.

I sat on the bed for what felt like an age, not knowing what to do. Then I looked back at the mirror, and noticed that my feet were visible. And then, my legs. Then, my body. And finally, my head. I was visible again! Or had the drugs worn off? I didn't care.

"Yes! Yes! Yes! I'm visible!" I yelled.

"Hello?" the locksmith shouted from the next room. "Is someone there?"

"I couldn't find you," he said when I walked back into the living room.

"Sorry about that. I was—err—under the bed." What else was I supposed to say?

"Under the bed?"

"Yeah. I lost an earring."

"Under the bed?"

"Yeah."

"I looked everywhere for you," he said. "And I shouted."

"Sorry, I didn't see or hear you. I was—"

"Under the bed?"

"Yeah."

He continued to give me strange looks while he replaced the lock. Who could blame him? He obviously thought I was some kind of nut job. I had him change the lock on the French doors too—just to be safe. The bill came to over a hundred pounds—it was money I could ill afford, but it was that or never get a good night's sleep again.

"Thanks again," I called after him. He'd no doubt be telling everyone back at his office about the crazy woman who had been hiding under the bed.

I dragged the book out from under the sofa. What on earth had just happened? I'd always considered myself to be a logical type of person, and every ounce of logic in me said that it wasn't possible to make yourself invisible.

But what other explanation could there be? I could have been drugged. Another possibility was that someone was trying to spook me, and had paid the locksmith to pretend he couldn't see me. But what about Mr Ivers? They might have paid him too. Or maybe they had told him it was a practical joke. None of that explained why I couldn't see my reflection in the mirror. Maybe someone had swapped the mirror for some kind of stage prop. Or maybe I was just going insane. Right now, that sounded like the sanest explanation.

I heard a noise coming from the bedroom—it was the same noise I'd heard earlier. I'd just about had enough of this.

"Don't be afraid," the woman said. At least I thought it was a woman. The figure appeared to float in mid-air between the bed and the wall. Her body was barely visible and her head seemed to be fading in and out of view. She said something which I could barely make out. It sounded like 'You're a witch'.

I closed my eyes, and took a deep breath. It was all in my head—just an overactive imagination—nothing more than that. Everything would be back to normal once I'd calmed down. Another deep breath, and then I'd open my eyes. Ready, breathe in, steady, breathe out, open eyes.

Phew! There was nothing there—obviously.

I found the number, which was still on my call log. She answered on the second ring.

"Aunt Lucy? It's Jill."

"Jill. How nice to hear your voice."

"We need to talk."

"Of course. I'll be happy to answer any questions you may have about your mother."

"This isn't about my mother. Well, it might be, I'm not sure. It would be better if we could talk face-to-face."

"Of course. Why don't you come over to Candlefield? I can answer your questions, and you'll have a chance to meet—"

"No!" I hadn't meant to shout, but there was no way I wanted to go back there. "Can you come to me? Could we meet in a coffee shop?"

"I don't really drink coffee."

"They have tea and soft drinks."

"A cup of tea would be lovely. When did you have in mind?"

"The sooner the better. How about tomorrow morning. Could you get to Washbridge by ten o'clock?"

She said that wasn't a problem, so I gave her the name of a coffee shop, which was close to my office.

I'd been trying to contact Mr Lyon, the husband of the first victim for some time, but without any success. He'd moved out of the family home. Only the police who were working on the case knew where he was staying, and they weren't likely to share that information with me. I did have a phone number, which I'd obtained from one of my contacts, but I had no idea whether Mr Lyon would still be using that number. I'd tried to call him numerous times, but he hadn't answered and he didn't have voice-mail activated. I decided to try one more time before calling it a day.

"Hello?" a man's voice said.

"Is that Mr Lyon?"

"Speaking."

"Mr Lyon. I'm sorry to bother you. I'm not the press." After my initial run-in with Mr Lamb, I thought I'd better make that clear. "My name is Jill Gooder, and I'm a private investigator."

"I was expecting your call."

"You were?"

"Harry Lamb mentioned that you'd been to see him."

"You're in touch with Mr Lamb?"

"Yes. We've met a couple of times. He said that you were investigating another murder, and that you thought it might be the same killer."

"I don't know for sure. Have you heard about the Caroline Fox case?"

"Only what I've seen in the papers. I mentioned it to the officer dealing with my wife's murder, but he insisted the cases were not connected."

"He could be right." There's a first time for everything.

"But you obviously don't think so or you wouldn't be calling me."

"I think it's at least worth exploring the possibility that the murders are connected. That's why I've been trying to contact you."

"I haven't been taking calls—most of them have been from the press. The only calls I've answered are from numbers I recognise. Harry Lamb gave me your number earlier today."

"Would it be possible for me to come and see you?"

"How about tomorrow morning?"

Oh bum, I'd arranged to meet Aunt Lucy then. "I have a meeting in the morning. Could we make it early afternoon? Say one o'clock?"

Mr Lyon confirmed that was okay, and gave me directions to the small hotel where he was staying.

Chapter 9

"I'm going to strangle you!" Mrs V shouted.

I heard her as soon as I walked into the building. It didn't take a genius to know what was going on. I hurried up the stairs and pushed open the door to find Winky sitting on top of the stationery cupboard. He looked as cool as a cucumber as he stared down with his one eye at Mrs V. Her face was so red it looked as if she might explode at any moment.

"I'm going to kill him." She had a knitting needle in her hand and looked as though she meant business.

I didn't need to ask why she was so angry. The floor was covered in wool of every colour. The mail sack, which usually housed the yarn, had been upended. Judging by the devastation in front of me, I guessed that Winky must have done it some hours ago before Mrs V arrived. Since then, he'd been playing with the numerous balls of wool, which had unravelled and were now entangled with one another. It looked like an explosion in a woolly jumper factory. I was struggling to keep a straight face. If I laughed, Mrs V would probably turn the knitting needle on me.

"Get him down, so I can kill him!" she yelled.

I walked over to the stationery cupboard, grabbed Winky, and then threw him into my office and closed the door.

"Let me at him!"

I put my body between her and the door. Obviously, I had some kind of death wish. "I'll help you to tidy up," I offered.

"Move out of the way! I'm going to kill him!"

"He was only playing."

Mrs V glared at me for the longest moment, and then took a step back. "Why can't you take him home with you, Jill? You know he hates me."

"I'm sure that isn't true." It was. "How about I buy you a linen basket with a catch on it? You can keep all your yarn in there and it'll be safe from Winky."

"Can I at least give him a kick up the backside?"

"No."

"Just a tap?"

"No."

So much for catching up on my paperwork. We managed to unravel and rewind most of the wool by the time I had to leave for my meeting with Aunt Lucy. I made Mrs V promise that she wouldn't throw Winky out of the window while I was out, and I promised to buy her a linen basket.

I poked my head around the door of my office. Winky was lying on my desk looking completely unfazed by the morning's events. I poured him a saucer of milk—full cream—and gave him some cat food.

"Behave while I'm out," I said as I turned to leave.

"Okay."

I spun around.

"Meow. Meow."

I really needed a holiday.

I was ten minutes late arriving at the coffee shop. I'd arranged to meet Aunt Lucy outside, but there was no sign of her. I doubted she'd have left because she had been really keen for us to meet. As I stepped inside, I wasn't even sure if I'd recognise her, but I needn't have worried. Her outfit spanned the colour spectrum. Red shoes with pink tights. A green skirt with a bright yellow blouse. Blue cats' eyes glasses, orange lipstick and dark green hair. She was obviously going for *understated*.

"Jill!" She waved at me from across the room. "Jill! I'm over here!"

I could sense everyone was staring at me—no doubt wondering who could possibly be meeting the crazy, rainbow lady. Aunt Lucy already had a pot of tea and a slice of cake on the table in front of her, so I gave her a little wave to let her know I'd seen her, and then went to the counter to order myself a coffee.

"Sorry I'm late."

"Don't worry your head, dear." Aunt Lucy's smile was almost too wide for her face. "Lovely to see you again. Sit down, sit down." She patted the seat next to her, but I took the chair opposite.

"I can't drink coffee." She pointed to my latte. "It doesn't agree with me. I prefer tea. Camomile preferably. They have some lovely cakes in here. I just couldn't resist. Would you like a taste?"

"No, thanks. I'm good."

"My daughters, your cousins, Amber and Pearl run a small cake shop and tea room. They sell the most delicious cupcakes. You really should come over and—"

"I have a few questions." I was in no mood to discuss my cupcake baking cousins.

"Of course, my dear. Fire away." Aunt Lucy polished off the last of the cake, and licked the spoon.

"The book," I said in little more than a whisper.

"You mean the book of spells?"

"Yes. Why did you send it to me?"

"Your mother wanted you to have it."

"What am I supposed to do with it? It's just nonsense."

Aunt Lucy smiled. "You know that's not true."

"There's no such thing as spells or magic." I was still convinced that there had to be a logical explanation for the events of the previous evening.

"My dear, of course there is." Aunt Lucy took a sip of her tea, and placed her hand on mine. My instinct was to pull away, but there was something strangely comforting about her touch. "Do you remember what your mother said before she passed?"

How could I forget? I wasn't sure if I'd ever forgive that last act of cruelty. "She must have hated me."

"That's not true. Your mother loved you more than life itself."

"Then why did she call me a witch? With her dying breath!"

"It was important to her that you knew."

"Knew what?"

"That you *are* a witch."

I pulled my hand away.

"What's wrong, Jill?"

"What's wrong? You call me a witch, and then ask what's wrong? What do you think is wrong?"

"Jill, please. I don't think you understand."

"What's there to understand? You called me a witch! Why come all of this way just to insult me?"

I started to get up, but Aunt Lucy grabbed my hand. Her grip was surprisingly strong.

"This is a waste of time." I tried to pull away.

"Please, Jill. Hear me out. Then, if you still want to leave, I won't try to stop you."

I tried to pull away, but I couldn't break her grip.

"Please, Jill. Sit down."

"Okay, but this had better be good."

"I want to show you something—if that's okay?"

I shrugged.

She pushed the empty plate, which had held the cake, into the centre of the table. Then she closed her eyes.

"There," she said.

I'd been so focussed on Aunt Lucy, that it took me a few seconds to realise that the cake, which I'd seen her eat, was now back on the plate.

"That's the 'take it back' spell." She pulled the plate closer to herself, and began to eat the cake—again.

"How did you do that?" It was a clever trick. She must have had two slices. I checked under the table, but couldn't see a second plate.

"I know this is difficult for you to accept." Aunt Lucy wiped a smudge of chocolate from the corner of her mouth. "But please try. When your mother said '*you're a witch*', it wasn't to be hurtful. It wasn't an insult. It was because you really are a witch."

"Sure I am. I suppose you are too?"

Aunt Lucy nodded. "Our whole family are witches. Your mother, your grandma and your cousins."

"There's no such thing as witches! You're crazy."

"How else do you explain this?" She took another spoonful of cake.

"I don't know. It must be some kind of trick."

"What about the spell you cast last night?"

"I didn't cast a spell," I lied.

"So you didn't make yourself invisible?"

How could she have known? Unless she'd been inside my flat. "I didn't. I wasn't."

"I felt the force when you did it," Aunt Lucy said. "I'd been waiting and hoping I would."

"It was some kind of elaborate illusion." I was running out of straws to clutch at. "Did you pay the locksmith to pretend he couldn't see me?"

"Sooner or later you are going to have to accept this."

"That's never going to happen. Look, if I really am a witch." I scoffed. "How come I've gone all my life without knowing it? How come I haven't turned anyone into a frog or something?"

"When you were born, it wasn't safe for your mother to keep you with her."

I wanted to ask why not, but knew I'd get the same old *it's complicated* nonsense, so I allowed her to continue.

"Before she gave you up for adoption, your mother cast a spell that effectively blocked your powers. That spell remained in place until she died. When she knew she had only hours to live, she reached out to you. She wanted you to know before she passed away."

"I don't know what you expect me to say. You're asking me to believe in magic and witches. I just can't."

"Have you noticed anything else unusual since your mother died?"

"No."

"Are you sure?"

I recalled the surge of energy I'd felt when my mother died, but surely that was just the shock of what had happened. Then there was Winky. But that had just been my over-active imagination—cats can't talk. And then there was the strange, ghostly figure in my bedroom. I'd just been over-tired.

"I'm sure. Nothing at all."

I could see Aunt Lucy didn't believe me, but at that point I really didn't care. "I probably should be going."

"Why don't you pay another visit to Candlefield?"

"I can't take time off work. I'm busy."

"You wouldn't need to take time off. Time in this world will stand still while you're in Candlefield."

This was a whole new level of crazy. I wasn't even going to try to get my head around such nonsense. Still, Candlefield was a beautiful village.

"If I did come, could I bring Kathy?"

"I'm afraid that's not possible."

"But she's my sister."

"I know, and I'm sorry, but it's simply not possible."

"Why not?"

"Candlefield is home to sups only."

"Soups? What do you mean?"

"Sups, not soups. It's shorthand. A collective term for supernatural beings: witches, vampires, werewolves—"

"Whoa! Right there! Now you're trying to tell me there are vampires and werewolves? Okay, that's it!" I stood up. "I'm done here."

"Jill, wait!" Aunt Lucy reached out to me, but this time I was determined to leave. There was only so much crazy anyone could take in a day.

I could hear her calling after me as I walked down the high street, but I had no intention of stopping. After five minutes of power walking, her voice had faded into the distance. At her age, she had no hope of keeping up with me. I slowed my pace and tried to get my bearings. The hotel where Mr Lyon was staying was no more than half a mile away. I'd be early, but it was worth a try. If he wasn't in or couldn't see me yet, I could always wait in the lobby.

Werewolves? Vampires? Just how gullible did she think I was? The idea that Kathy couldn't go to Candlefield because she was human — it was laughable.

"Jill."

I almost jumped out of my skin when Aunt Lucy stepped out of a shop doorway in front of me. How had she done that? I thought I'd left her way behind — there was no way she could have made up that distance. She must have hailed a taxi. She was persistent, I'd give her that much.

"I have nothing more to say to you." I tried to side-step her, but she was quicker than I expected in blocking my path.

"This is important," she said.

"What is?"

"I know you aren't ready to accept this yet — "

"That I'm a witch? — I'll never be ready to accept that nonsense!"

"There's one thing you have to know. The main reason your mother gave you up was because she feared for your life."

"Why?"

"It's difficult to explain."

"Let me guess. It's complicated?"

"All I ask is that you be on your guard. If you sense danger then trust your instincts and get away as quickly as possible."

"Okay, fine." I'd heard enough. "Now, I really have to go."

I began to walk away.

"Your mother is looking out for you too. Make sure you heed her warnings."

"My mother?" What was that supposed to mean? My mother was dead. I turned back to face Aunt Lucy, but she was nowhere to be seen.

Chapter 10

When I arrived at the hotel, the receptionist informed me that Mr Lyon had gone out. He'd said he'd be back after lunch. I could have gone back to the office, but I couldn't face that pantomime, so I decided to pass the time by looking for a linen basket for Mrs V.

"Can I help you, madam?" An over eager young sales assistant asked. "We have several different sizes of basket."

"Yes, so I see."

"Does madam have a lot of linen?"

"It's not actually for linen."

"Oh?"

"It's for yarn. Wool. To keep it safe." Maybe if I smiled, she wouldn't think I was totally crazy.

"Yarn?" She looked confused. My smile hadn't fooled her; she obviously thought I was wacko.

"My receptionist likes to knit—a lot. Scarves mainly."

"I see." She obviously didn't, and who could blame her?

"And you want to keep the wool safe?"

"From Winky."

"Winky?"

"My cat. He lives at the office. He's only got one eye."

"Right." She smiled, and began to edge away. "Give me a shout if you need any help."

Judging by the speed at which she left, I doubted that she'd respond to a request for further assistance. She was probably on her way to warn security to keep an eye on the mad woman who wanted a linen basket to keep yarn safe from her one-eyed cat. When you put it like that—I guess it did sound a little crazy.

The hotel receptionist wasn't overly thrilled at having to store my linen basket for me. That was until I mentioned Winky. It turned out she was a cat lover, and suddenly nothing was too much trouble.

Geoffrey Lyon was back in his room. Fourth floor – room four one five.

"Come in." He greeted me at the door. Although younger than Mr Lamb, he looked even more tired and drawn. The room was as predictable and depressing as most budget-priced hotels.

"Drink? I only have whiskey I'm afraid." He gestured to a half-empty bottle on the coffee table.

"No thanks. I'm good." After my morning, I'd have killed for a drink, but I needed to stay focussed. "Thank you for agreeing to see me."

"Grab a seat." He pointed to one of two threadbare chairs. "You don't mind if I do, do you?" He picked up the bottle.

"No, go ahead."

After he'd topped up his glass, he took a seat next to me. "This place is a dump, but I had to get away from the house."

"Press?"

"Nah. I can deal with them. It's just–" He appeared lost in his thoughts. "All the memories. I can't bear it."

I nodded – unsure what to say.

"Harry Lamb tells me you think Pauline's murder might be connected to others," he said at last.

"It's only a theory at the moment, but one I believe is worth following up."

"It's more than the police are doing."

"I'm sure they're doing their best." Why was I sticking

up for Jack Maxwell and his cronies?

"I wish I shared your faith in them. What can I do to help?"

"Can we start with the day of the murder? Where were you when it happened?"

"I'd been to visit my mother. She's in a nursing home. Been there a few months now. I'm not sure she'll ever come out."

"Sorry to hear that." The image of my mother on her deathbed flashed across my mind. "Your wife didn't go with you?"

"No. She and my mother didn't see eye to eye. They hadn't seen one another for over five years. There was some kind of silly falling out. I can't even remember what it was about."

He seemed to zone out again. I waited for a few seconds and then prompted him, "When you got back?"

"I found her lying on the bedroom floor. There was blood everywhere." He began to cry. "Who would do such a thing? Why would anyone want to kill her?"

"Can you think of any reason why someone would have done this?"

"No. That's why I reckon there might be something in your serial killer theory. Maybe it *is* some psycho who has decided to kill women based upon their names."

"How was she on the days leading up to the murder? Did you notice any change in her?"

"No. She was the same old Pauline. Except for the reunion thing."

"What reunion thing?"

"It was nothing, really. She'd been looking forward to her school's reunion for months, but then at the last minute, she cancelled."

"Did she say why?"

"She said she was ill, but—"

"You don't sound convinced."

He finished off the last few drops of whiskey. "She said she was feeling under the weather, and didn't feel up to going, but then she went out anyway—to visit her sister."

"When was that?"

"Two days before—" He broke down again.

We talked for almost an hour. When I left, I promised to keep him posted of any new development. In turn, he promised to contact me if he thought of anything else that might be relevant.

"I had to throw four balls of wool away." Mrs V greeted me with this when I struggled into the office—linen basket in tow. "They were too tangled to sort out."

"Everything will be okay now you have this." I slid the basket across the floor until it was next to the mail sack.

"When you transfer the wool from the mail sack," Mrs V said, "make sure you keep the same colours together."

"You want *me* to transfer the yarn?"

"That's very kind of you, dear."

Did I have *mug* written on my forehead? "I am kind of busy."

"Me too, dear." She held up her current knitting project—a black and purple scarf. Obviously that took precedence over a little thing like a serial killer investigation. This was no doubt my punishment for insisting that Winky stay at the office.

"There you go!" I pointed to the linen basket, which was now full of yarn. "That's better isn't it?"

"I suppose it will have to do until you get rid of that stupid cat."

So ungrateful. "Did you remember to feed Winky?"

Mrs V gave me one of her looks.

"Not to worry. I'll do it now."

Winky was all over me like a rash the moment I walked into my office.

"Look buddy," I said. "I need to know something." I glanced back to make sure Mrs V hadn't followed me. The coast was clear so I crouched down next to him. "Can you or can you not talk?"

"Meow, meow."

"Do you want this?" I held up a can of chicken and sardine mix.

"Meow, meow."

"Go on, ask me for it then."

"Meow, meow."

What had I expected? Of course the stupid cat couldn't talk.

"Meow, meow."

"Okay, okay." I scooped it into his dish, and then gave him milk from the fridge—full cream, obviously.

This is what it had come to. I was asking the cat to talk to me. I sat on the leather sofa and watched Winky devour his food. My conversation with Aunt Lucy kept spinning around in my head—one thing in particular. What had she called them? Sups? According to her, all manner of supernatural creatures lived in Candlefield. Even if I bought into the idea of witches and magic—which I definitely didn't—not even a little bit. But even if I did, I was never going to believe there were such things as vampires, werewolves or whatever other make-believe creature she'd dreamed up.

According to Aunt Lucy, Kathy couldn't visit Candlefield because she was human. Well, we'd just have to see about that.

It took Kathy ages to pick up. "What?"

Something in her voice told me this was a bad time.

"It's me," I said. "Are you okay?"

"Sorry, Jill. I thought it was Pete. We had an argument this morning."

"What about?"

"I can't even remember. I just know I'm not talking to him. Whatever you do, don't get married."

"You're the one who's always trying to marry me off."

"Well don't marry Pete. He's a pig."

"You love him."

"I know I do. Doesn't mean he's not a pig. Why did you call?"

"Are you doing anything?"

"Only the ironing, what's up?"

"Fancy a drive out?"

"Where to?"

"Candlefield."

"Sure. I'd love to. Anything to escape the housework. Can you pick me up in twenty? I just need to ask Pete's mother to babysit the kids."

"Won't she mind?"

"Are you kidding? She's always asking if she can have them."

"Okay. See you in a bit. Oh, just one thing—"

"What?"

"Do you believe in werewolves?"

"What?"

"What about vampires?"

"Have you been at the bottle? Do you want me to drive?"

"It's okay. I'm sober." I laughed. "See you soon."

"Did Peter's mum come through?" I asked, as Kathy climbed into the passenger seat.

"Yeah. All sorted. So what's this all about? Aren't you supposed to be working on the serial killer case?"

"I am working on it, but I need to take a break for an hour or two. I thought you might like to see Candlefield. It really is beautiful."

"Is there a pub there? I could murder a drink."

"I didn't notice one, but I'm sure there will be."

"What was all that about werewolves and vampires?" Kathy asked.

"Nothing. Forget it."

I still had the hand-drawn map, which I'd used when I'd been to the funeral. Not that I expected to need it this time because I could remember exactly where the signpost and turn off to Candlefield were.

"How's the case going?" Kathy asked.

"I haven't made much progress, but then I have been rather distracted with everything that's happened recently. I did manage to interview the husbands of the first two victims though."

"Anything interesting?"

"Not really. There's no obvious motive for either killing. Both have the hallmarks of 'stranger' murder. I'm having difficulty tying either of them into the third murder."

"Your client's girlfriend?"

"Yeah. I could really do with seeing the police reports. According to that asshat Maxwell, the MOs of the first two murders are very different to the third."

"I'm sure if you were to ask Jack nicely —"

"I'd rather chew Winky's cat litter than have to go crawling to Jack Maxwell for anything."

"I suppose I'd better cancel the engagement party I booked for you and Jacky Boy then?" Kathy laughed.

I didn't.

I hit the brakes harder than I'd intended.

"What the?" Kathy looked back down the road. "What's up?"

"The sign."

"I don't see a sign."

"Exactly. It should have been half a mile back. Did you see it?"

"No, but then I wasn't really looking for it. We probably missed it when we were talking about the case."

I checked that the road was clear and did a U-turn.

"It should be up here on the right. Just after that bus stop."

We reached the bus stop, and continued at a crawl, but there was no signpost or turn-off.

"Are you sure we're on the right road?" Kathy said.

"I'm not stupid," I snapped. "Sorry. This is definitely the right road. It's only a few days since I was here. Take a look for yourself." I passed her the letter.

"At what?"

"The map on the back."

"It's blank." Kathy held up the letter. She was right.

I drove back and forth for another twenty minutes before giving up. On the way back home, I pulled into a pub called The Rainbow. Kathy thought it was hilarious that I'd been unable to find the road to Candlefield. I'd always given her such a hard time for her terrible sense of direction. I laughed it off, and agreed that I must have got the roads mixed up. What else was I supposed to say? I knew for sure that I'd been on the right road, and I knew precisely where the signpost and turn-off should have been. I desperately wanted to come up with some kind of logical explanation, but how on earth was I meant to explain this?

After a couple of drinks—I stuck to soda water, but promised myself something stronger when I got home—I dropped Kathy off at Peter's mother's house. Her mother-in-law invited me to join them for dinner, but I made an excuse. I wasn't in the mood.

"Thanks, sis," Kathy said as she climbed out of the car. "And don't worry about Candlefield. I'm sure it will turn up." She laughed at her own joke, and then hurried down the driveway.

The first thing I did when I got back to my flat was to pour myself a vodka. The second thing I did was to grab the book of spells, and take it to the skip. This time I double-checked that I'd locked my door. I went straight there and back. Even so, when I got back to the flat I hardly dared look inside. What if it had happened again?

What if the book was back on the coffee table? I took a deep breath and stepped inside.

Phew! There was nothing on the coffee table. I crouched down and checked under the sofa. Nothing. Thank goodness! Good riddance!

Chapter 11

The next morning, I woke up with a killer hangover. It was my own fault for having that second glass of vodka, but after the day I'd had yesterday, who could blame me? My eyes were barely open as I felt my way to the kitchen. After swallowing two aspirin, I staggered back into the living room.

I lay on the sofa waiting for the pain to subside. It was fifteen minutes before I could bear to open my eyes.

And, I wished I hadn't bothered. There on the coffee table was the book of spells.

"No!" I yelled at the thing. "No!" This could not be happening.

It was open at a spell called 'obscurer'. According to its description, the spell created a smoke shield, which could hide you for up to five minutes—long enough to get away.

Get away from what, I wondered.

"From the Dark One and his Followers," a woman's voice said.

The moment I heard the voice, my instincts took over. I jumped over the back of the sofa and crouched down.

"Jill," the woman said.

I recognised the voice. It was the same voice that had called me a witch.

"Jill, we need to talk."

This had to be a dream. A very bad dream. It must have been the vodka. I'd thought I was awake, but I was obviously still asleep.

"Jill. Please come out. We need to talk."

"Leave me alone!" I shouted. "Go away!" It was

obviously a figment of my imagination. I would stand up and prove to myself that it was all in my head. "One, two—two and a bit." Come on you coward. "One, two, three!"

I stood up.

"Hello, Jill," my dead mother said. "There's nothing to be afraid of."

She looked younger, and certainly healthier than the woman who I'd seen in the nursing home. Hold on. What was I saying? Younger and healthier? What about the small matter of her being dead? "You're not real," I said, holding onto the back of the sofa. "I saw you die."

"You did."

"How am I talking to you then? Are you a ghost or something?"

"That's right. I've tried to contact you a few times, but you seemed resistant. I'm glad you decided to let your guard down a little."

The vodka must have done that for me. Memo to self—one glass maximum from now on.

"Why don't you come and sit down?" My dead mother pointed a ghostly finger at the sofa I was still standing behind.

"I'm okay here, thanks."

"I don't bite."

"Nah. I think I'll stay where I am."

"As you wish." My mother glided across the room. As far as I could tell, her feet didn't actually touch the floor. They seemed to hover a few inches above it. She took a seat in the chair opposite the sofa. When I say 'took a seat' what I really mean is that she gave the appearance of being seated. On closer examination, I could see that she was actually hovering just above the seat.

"What do you want?" Why was I talking to a ghost?

"Just to talk."

"Why choose now to talk to me? Why didn't you — and I realise this might sound crazy. Why didn't you talk to me when you were still alive?"

"I had to protect you."

"And how exactly were you doing that by abandoning me?"

"It's —"

"Let me guess — *complicated*. That's what Aunt Lucy said. What does that mean exactly?"

"I'll explain everything, I promise, but for now it's important you know that I was always with you. I saw you almost every day."

"You did a great job of hiding then because I don't recall ever seeing you before that day at the nursing home."

"A witch has her ways."

"A witch?" Here we go again. "Of course. Silly me. I should have realised. I'd forgotten that you and the rest of my family are witches. You don't seriously expect me to believe that do you?"

"I think you already do."

"No I don't."

"It's okay to admit it. I know it must be scary coming out of the blue like this."

I walked slowly around the sofa and took a seat. "I don't know what to think. I don't know what's real and what isn't any more. Last week, I had a normal life. I went to work, I came home. All the usual things. And now this."

"I realise it's a lot for you to take in. A witch usually knows who she is from the moment she's born. This has all been dropped on you at once. There's no wonder you're confused."

"No kidding. How am I supposed to believe that things I thought existed only in books and movies are actually real? Witches, werewolves, vampires? Really?" I burst out laughing.

"What's funny?" she smiled.

"Oh nothing much. It's just that I'm having a conversation with a ghost who used to be a witch. How screwed up is that?"

"Things would be better if you'd agree to move to Candlefield. It would be much easier to protect you there."

"I'm not moving. My family—." I hesitated. "My *real family* are right here. So is my business."

Perhaps it was my imagination, but she seemed to flinch at the words '*real family*'. Good! I was glad. I wanted her to experience some of the pain I'd felt.

"I understand, and that's why it's even more important that you are aware of the dangers you're going to face."

I was parched. My tongue felt like sandpaper. "I need a cup of tea." I hesitated. "Can ghosts drink?" It was now official. I'd taken the leap into full blown crazy. Not only was I having a conversation with a ghost (who don't let's forget, used to be a witch), but I'd just asked her if she'd like a cup of tea.

"I'd love one."

"Really?" Not the response I'd expected. "You can drink?"

"And eat too. I wouldn't say no to a custard cream. I was pleased to see you keep your biscuits in separate containers."

"You too?" Maybe she was my mother after all.

"Of course. Your aunt Lucy always insists on mixing them up in that huge biscuit tin of hers. I'm sure she only does it because she knows I won't eat them once they've been mixed together. That means there's more for her."

"Just like Kathy."

"Your sister. Such a nice woman."

"You know her?"

"Of course. Like I said, I've watched you grow up. I couldn't have wished for a nicer family for you."

I put the tea and biscuits on the coffee table, and then settled back onto the sofa.

"I like what you've done with this place." She took a bite of biscuit. "I love the sixties theme."

"Thanks. Me too. How come I never saw you when I was growing up?"

"The 'invisible' spell, which I used when I was alive, made it impossible for you to know I was there. It's different now that I'm a ghost. I suspect you've already sensed my presence over the last few days."

I had, but at the time, I'd had no idea what it was. "So what happens now?" I sipped my tea. "Do you plan to haunt me?"

"Haunt? Such a nasty word. It sounds kind of threatening. I hope you don't find me threatening?"

Curiously, I didn't. After I'd got over the initial shock, I'd begun to relax. Why wouldn't I? After all, having tea and biscuits with an ex-witch, now-ghost was the most natural thing in the world.

"What would happen if Kathy walked in now? Would she be able to see you?"

"No. You're the only one who can see me. Ghosts have to 'attach' themselves to a living person in order for that person to see and hear them."

"So she'd think I was talking to myself?"

"Pretty much. But then she probably already thinks you're a little crazy after yesterday, doesn't she?"

I nodded. "I guess so. Why did the signpost and turn off to Candlefield disappear?"

"Can't you guess?"

"Because Kathy was with me in the car?"

"That's right. Only sups can go to Candlefield. Humans will never find their way there because effectively it doesn't exist in the human world. Even you needed a little help the first time you went—that's why Lucy provided you with a map."

"I still managed to get lost . I was late for—"

"My funeral?" She smiled. "The one you were late for?"

"I'm sorry."

"It's okay. It gave me a good laugh."

"You were there? At your own funeral?"

"Of course. The cakes afterwards were delicious."

"Can Aunt Lucy and the others see you too?"

"A ghost can only 'attach' itself to one living person at a time. If I need Lucy to see me, I'll have to break my attachment with you temporarily."

"I like Aunt Lucy, but I'm afraid I've been rather rude to her."

"Don't give it a second thought. Lucy understands what you're going through. We had a quick chat yesterday after you met her in the coffee shop."

I talked to my ex-witch, now-ghost mother for ages.

Most of the conversation revolved around my childhood. She'd been there for every significant event. I had to fight back the tears as I realised how much she really did care for me. All those years when I had thought I'd been abandoned, she'd been right there by my side. She remembered my first day at school, the day I slipped and broke my leg, and even my first kiss.

"I never did like Tommy Jacobs," she said.

"Neither did I." I laughed at the memory of me and Tommy kissing behind the bike sheds when I was fourteen. I'd wanted to know what it would be like to kiss a boy, and he'd been a willing volunteer.

"Your taste in men hasn't improved much since then."

"That's not true." It so was.

"It's time you found yourself a nice young man and settled down."

Something suddenly occurred to me. "If what you say is true, and I am a witch. Can I still marry a—"

"Human? Of course you can, but you won't be able to tell him you're a witch."

"Wouldn't he know?"

"It's every sup's responsibility to ensure that humans never find out we exist. It is the single most important thing you must do. If a human was to find out, their life would be in danger."

"So I can't tell Kathy?"

"You mustn't tell any human. That's why it would be much easier if you moved to Candlefield."

"I can't do that. Do other sups live outside of Candlefield?"

"Of course."

"So, there are witches, vampires, werewolves and other

sups living among us here in Washbridge?"

"Yes. The number of sups who live outside of Candlefield is relatively low, but they can be found everywhere in the human world. Now that you have inherited your powers, you'll find that identifying them is much easier."

"How will I recognise them?"

"It's difficult to explain. You just will. Not all sups allow themselves to be revealed though. Some choose to obscure their true identity. You must be on your guard at all times."

"From what exactly?"

She went on to explain precisely why she'd given me up for adoption. The most evil sup of all was known as The Dark One. No one knew who he was or even what type of sup he was: werewolf, vampire, wizard or something else. His true identity was a mystery. He was extremely powerful, and had a small army of supporters who were known simply as Followers.

"Does this *Dark One* live in Candlefield?"

"No one knows for sure."

"If no one knows who or what he is, how do you even know he exists?"

"He exists."

"Why does he want to kill me?"

"You come from a long line of witches. A line more powerful than any other. The Dark One wants to claim that power for himself. If he were ever able to do so, he'd become unstoppable."

"Did he kill you?"

"Someone or something managed to breach my defences and mortally wound me. He couldn't have done it alone, but I believe he may have orchestrated it. That's why I had to make contact with you, so I could pass on the power before he could claim it for himself."

I remembered the energy I'd felt at my mother's bedside at the moment she'd passed away. Was that her power passing to me? I was silent for a while as I allowed it all to sink in.

"Can I really do all the magic spells in this book?" I sat forward on the sofa and began to page through the book of spells.

"With practice, yes. Would you like to try a few now?"

Chapter 12

"Can anyone cast these spells?" I said. "If they knew the sequence of images, I mean. If I asked Kathy to picture the mental images for the 'invisible' spell, would it work for her?"

"No." My mother shook her ghostly head. "They will only work for a witch. If your sister or any other human tried to cast the spell by picturing the images, nothing would happen. The images are just a key that unlocks and focuses your magic."

"Where should I begin?" I was overwhelmed by the sheer number of spells.

"I'd suggest you start with something easy. How about the 'take it back' spell."

"Aunt Lucy did that one in the coffee shop yesterday — on a piece of cake. I thought it was some kind of sleight of hand."

"You'll find it on page thirty seven."

I paged through until I found it. The description said the spell would take an object back in time. It warned that it would work only on objects, not on living creatures, and would take the object back ten minutes in time.

"So I couldn't send a person back in time?" I said.

"No. It won't work on any living being. Why don't you try it on the plate?"

The plate in front of me was now empty except for a sprinkling of crumbs. We'd made short work of the custard creams.

"Okay. Why not?" I was beginning to feel excited about the whole 'witch' thing.

Thankfully, the list of mental images required was quite

short because I felt a little self-conscious with my mother watching. When I'd completed the final instruction, I stared at the plate, but nothing had happened. There was no sign of the biscuits.

"I must have done it wrong." I began again. This time, I really concentrated on the sequence of images. The plate was still empty. "I'm useless." I sighed.

My mother laughed.

"Are you sure I'm your daughter? Maybe there was a mix up at the adoption agency?"

"I'm sure." She took another biscuit out of the Tupperware box and put it on the plate. "Eat that," she said.

I didn't need telling twice to eat a custard cream. I could eat them from morning until night.

"Right," she said, after I'd polished off the biscuit. "Try the spell again."

By now I'd lost all confidence, but went through the motions anyway. As soon as I'd finished the last instruction, the biscuit reappeared on the plate.

"I don't get it," I said, as I picked it up—just to check it was real.

"Read the description of the spell again."

I did—taking my time over every word. "Ten minutes!" I said, louder than I'd intended.

"Precisely. The spell will only take the object back ten minutes in time. You ate the other biscuits much longer ago, so taking the object back ten minutes had no effect."

"I'm an idiot. Sorry."

"It doesn't matter. I just wanted to illustrate the importance of reading the description of every spell carefully. There's no point in being able to perform a spell if you're expecting it to do something it wasn't designed to do."

I picked up the book of spells. "This thing weighs a ton! Can I get a digital version or an audio book?"

"You young people." My mother laughed. "It's only available in hard copy, I'm afraid. And, it's the first of many you will have to master. This is just level one."

"Level one? How many levels are there?"

"You don't need to worry about that right now. Just focus on mastering every spell in this book."

I flicked through the pages again. "All of them?"

She nodded. "I suggest you learn a few each day."

The thought of having to learn every spell was daunting, and yet I was excited. "Can I try another?"

"Of course. Try as many as you like. The book belongs to you now."

I flicked through the pages again. "What about this one?"

"Why not?"

The spell was called 'lightning bolt'. I made sure to read the description really carefully this time.

"Are you sure it's safe to try this one in the flat?"

"Provided you select your target carefully."

I knew just the thing. My last boyfriend had been a total loser — one in a long line of losers. When I'd finally had enough and told him it was over, he'd sent me a large stuffed cow with a note on it that had read 'A cow for a cow'. Charmer eh? I'd put it in my wardrobe and more or less forgotten about it, but now was the perfect time to bring it out again.

"You'd better put it on the hob," my mother advised. "The splash guard will prevent you from damaging the paintwork."

Once the cow was on the hob, I went back into the living room to get the book. To my surprise my mother had disappeared, but when I stepped back into the kitchen, she was seated on one of the stools.

"Okay. Here goes nothing." I took a deep breath.

Once again I worked my way through the sequence of images. This was far more complicated than the 'invisible' spell. The final instruction read 'point the middle finger of your right hand at the target'.

The blast almost knocked me off my feet. A lightning bolt shot out of the tip of my finger and struck the cow in the centre of its belly. What had once been a stuffed cow was now a smouldering heap of cloth and stuffing.

"Wow! That was fantastic." I studied my fingertip, half expecting to see a burn mark, but there wasn't even the slightest blemish.

"You must use all of the spells with great care."

"I will." Even as I made the promise, I had an image of Jack Maxwell on the wrong end of my lightning bolt.

My mother stood up from the stool. "It's time I was leaving. This ghost stuff is all still new to me. I find that making myself visible for any length of time can be exhausting."

"When will I see you again?"

"Don't worry. I'll be around. Just be on your guard and make sure you keep an eye open for anything suspicious."

Before I could reply, she'd disappeared.

Holy moly. I was a witch. An actual witch. I desperately wanted to tell someone, but I couldn't. Normally, Kathy would have been the first person to have heard my news, but I wasn't allowed to tell her because she was a mere human. Pah! Humans—ten-a-penny. It's all about the witches! It was probably just as well that I couldn't tell her. What kind of reaction would I have got? She'd have probably put in a call to the men in white coats.

It would have been nice to spend more time practising spells, but it was already mid-morning. Mrs V would be wondering where I was. I'd left my phone in the bedroom, and sure enough when I checked, there were three missed calls—all from Mrs V.

"It's me," I said.

"Jill? Are you okay? I was beginning to worry when you didn't answer your phone."

"Yeah. I'm okay now. I had a bit of an iffy tummy overnight, so I slept in. My phone was in my coat pocket, so I didn't hear your calls." I hated lying to Mrs V, but what else was I supposed to do? She'd have disapproved of the hangover, and I could hardly tell her that I'd been practising spells with the help of my mother's ghost.

"Anything I need to know about?"

"That stupid cat has got himself caught up in the blinds again."

Not again. Winky loved to sit on the window sill, but would occasionally get carried away and launch himself at a bird that was flying past the window. That usually only resulted in a sore head when he crashed into the glass, but occasionally he'd get tangled in the blinds.

"Did you get him out?"

"No."

"Is he still stuck there?"

"Just a minute." I heard her place the phone onto the desk. Next, I heard her open the door into my office, and then slam it closed again. "No. Looks like he got himself out."

"Is he okay?"

There was silence on the other end, and I realised Mrs V was probably shrugging.

"Okay. Well I'm on my way. Anything else I should know?"

"You had a call from Mr Peterson. He wanted to know if you had any news for him."

"What did you say?"

"I said I didn't know. I asked him if he had any idea how to free a cat from a blind."

I cringed. "What did he say?"

"He said he didn't, but that he'd like you to contact him with an update."

"Okay. See you soon."

I was going nowhere fast with this investigation, but then in my defence it wasn't every day that you discovered you were a witch, and had a visit from your mother's ghost. Not that I could tell Danny Peterson that.

Spells are addictive. After I'd showered and dressed, I started for the door, but my gaze was drawn to the book. Maybe I had time for one more before I left for work. Something quick and simple. I flicked through the pages looking for those with the least number of images to be memorised. Eventually, about two-thirds of the way through the book, I found one with only five images. It was one of the shortest I'd seen. Titled 'faster', it allowed you to move at what it described as 'breakneck speed' in short bursts. Hmm, interesting—that could come in handy. I read it through a few times until I was confident

I had it memorised. After sliding the book under the sofa, I made my way out into the corridor. I did a quick check to make sure no one was around, and then I cast the spell. Nothing happened. Had I visualised the images out of sequence? There wasn't time to go back and check, so I began to walk down the corridor. The next thing I knew I was standing next to my car. Wow! I hadn't made a mistake with the spell. It just hadn't taken effect until I had started to walk. This was wild.

"Afternoon," Mrs V greeted me. I took the sarcasm on the chin—I deserved it.
"Sorry about this morning. Iffy tummy."
"Alcohol can do that."
The woman knew me too well. No point in arguing—I never was a good liar.
"What do you think?" She held up her latest project. A red and white striped scarf.
"Very nice." It was hard to get excited about yet another scarf.
"Don't forget to call Mr Peterson."
"I won't, but I'd better check on Winky first."
Mrs V harrumphed her disapproval.
Winky didn't look happy, but when did he ever? He was perched on my desk as usual. I glanced at the blind and could see small tufts of fur stuck between the slats. That must have hurt.
"When are you ever going to learn?"
"If that stupid woman had got me out, I wouldn't have lost my fur."
"You can speak?"
"Of course I can speak."

"You can speak."

"You said that already. Now why don't you sack that useless old woman, and bring in a pretty young thing who loves cats?"

My mother had mentioned that I might notice other changes now that I'd inherited a witch's powers. This must be one of them. I wasn't going crazy after all.

"Well?" Winky demanded. "Are you going to sack the old bag?"

"No. And you mustn't call her that. Mrs V is a sweet thing."

"Sweet? Are you kidding? She hates me."

"You make it easy to hate you."

"What do you mean?"

"Look at the way you treat me, and I rescued you."

"Whoa. Just hold on. What do you mean you rescued me? I was the one who chose you. You should be honoured. I could have chosen anyone."

"*You* chose *me*?"

"Of course. Why else would I be here? And it's high time you showed me a little more gratitude — starting with the occasional tin of salmon. Red not pink. Obviously."

"Obviously."

"I'm glad we've got that sorted." He licked his lips. "Now where's that salmon?"

"This way, sir."

Winky followed me across the room.

"What do you call that?" he said when I emptied a can of cat food into his dish.

"It's called 'like it or lump it'."

I made a call to Danny Peterson.

"I'm sorry I haven't been in touch before now. Things have been a bit hectic."

"Any more news?"

"Nothing so far. I've spoken to the husbands of the first two victims, and there is nothing obvious to connect those murders to that of your girlfriend."

"That's just the point isn't it? The only connection is the name. He chose Caroline because her name was Fox."

"He?"

"Aren't all serial killers men?"

"Most," I conceded. "I still have a couple more people to talk to. I'll keep you posted."

Caroline Fox had no immediate family, so I decided to call in at her place of work. Maybe her work colleagues could give me more information about her. Danny had actually told me very little other than the two of them were in love and had planned to get engaged.

Caroline had worked at Washbridge Travel, a small, local travel agent on the outskirts of the town. I didn't bother to make an appointment—I didn't want to give them an opportunity to refuse to see me.

"Good afternoon, madam." The young woman with flamingo earrings, and an overdose of tan greeted me as soon as I walked through the door.

I'd known it was a small, independent concern, but I hadn't realised just how small. In the main shop there were only two desks. At the rear was a glass-fronted office.

"Good afternoon," I said.

"I'm Beth. Is there anything in particular I can help you with today?"

"Actually, Beth, I'm not here to book a holiday. I'd like to ask you a few questions about Caroline Fox."

Beth's smile evaporated. "Caroline?"

"My name is Jill Gooder. I'm a private investigator. I've been hired to look into Caroline's murder."

"Poor Caroline." The woman seemed visibly shaken. "Do you mind if I sit down?"

"Of course. Shall I get you a drink or something?"

"No, I'm okay. It's all so horrible. I still can't understand why anyone would do something like that. Caroline was such a lovely person."

"Were you and she close friends?"

"Not friends exactly. We didn't see each other outside of work, but we did get on really well. Everyone liked her."

"Do you know Danny Peterson, her boyfriend?"

"No, not really. Poor man. How's he taking it?"

"Pretty much as you'd expect. Did you know she was going to get engaged?"

"Engaged? Really? No, she hadn't mentioned it."

"Don't you think that's a little odd?"

"Yeah, I suppose. She did tend to keep her personal life to herself, but I'd have expected her to tell me about that."

"Had you noticed any change in her over the last few weeks?"

"Not really."

"Nothing at all? Are you sure?"

"She had seemed much happier recently. I don't know why. Maybe it was the engagement?"

"Maybe. Is there anything you can think of which might help me?"

"What kind of thing?"

"Anything. Did she mention any trouble or problems she was having? Had there been any disgruntled customers?"

"No, nothing like that. She might have said something to Graham." Beth gestured to the man seated in the office. "He's the manager. He and Caroline had a really good working relationship."

"Thanks." I handed her my card. "Please give me a call if you think of anything else.

Graham Tyler was in his early thirties.

"I don't understand what you're doing here exactly," he said. "Who are you working for?"

"Caroline's boyfriend, Danny Peterson. Do you know him?"

He hesitated for a moment too long. "Caroline may have mentioned him in passing, but that was some time ago."

"They were about to get engaged."

Tyler's expression changed—he looked puzzled. "Engaged? Are you sure?"

"Danny showed me the ring."

Tyler shrugged. I had the sense he was holding something back.

"She hadn't mentioned the engagement to you?" I pressed.

"No. Why would she? We were just work colleagues."

"Beth said you and Caroline had a good relationship."

He glared out through the glass at Beth who was still dabbing her eyes. "Caroline and I had a good *business* relationship. She was a good employee—that's all."

"Did Caroline say or do anything in the days leading up to her death that was in any way out of the ordinary?"

"Nothing at all." His voice faltered a little. "She seemed perfectly happy. "
"Okay. Well if you do think of anything else, please give me a call."

One other person who might have been able to give me more background on Caroline was her flatmate, Josie Trent. She was a dancer who had been working on a cruise liner for the previous few months, and wasn't due back in the country for several more weeks. She'd been somewhere off the coast of Barbados at the time Caroline was murdered. I'd tried a couple of times to contact her, but so far with no luck.
Josie was still on my 'to-do' list.

Chapter 13

It wasn't difficult to track down Mrs Lyon's sister, Janet Wesley. She lived alone in a flat on the north side of Washbridge.

"Yes?" She'd cracked open the door only as wide as the chain would allow.

"Mrs Wesley? I'm Jill Gooder. I spoke to your brother-in-law—"

"You're the private investigator?"

I nodded. "I'm sorry to trouble you. I wondered if I might have a word?"

She was already undoing the chain. "Geoff told me that he'd spoken to you. Do come in. Ignore the mess."

Janet Wesley was a woman after my own heart. Her idea of 'a mess' was an empty cup on the coffee table. Other than that, the flat was immaculately clean and tidy. Maybe she could give Kathy a few tips. I refused her offer of a drink, and got right down to business.

"Geoffrey told me that Pauline came to see you two days before she was murdered," I said. "On the night she should have gone to her school reunion."

"That's right. Are you sure you won't have a drink?"

"No, thanks. She told Geoffrey she wasn't well enough to go to the reunion, and yet she still came over here to see you?"

"She wasn't ill. She just told Geoff that." Janet Wesley smiled—a sad smile. "Geoff is a darling. He loved my sister to bits, but he's still a man."

I nodded even though I wasn't really sure what she was getting at.

"He wouldn't have understood. He'd have thought she

was being silly."

"Understood what?"

"The real reason Pauline didn't go to the reunion. She'd been looking forward to it for months, but then some idiot made a complete pig's ear of her hair. She took a real pride in her appearance—especially her hair. She couldn't bear the idea of anyone seeing her like that. If Geoff had known that was why Pauline didn't want to go to the reunion, he'd have tried to persuade her to go anyway."

"What exactly happened to her hair?"

"She told me that the hairdresser had been drunk or high on drugs. Her hair looked as though it had been attacked by a lawn mower. When she complained, the manager of the salon stepped in, but by then the damage had already been done. The manager told her that the only way to rescue her hair was to cut it really short. Pauline hated to wear her hair short; she didn't think it suited her, but she had no other option. She was distraught when she came to see me."

"Geoffrey didn't mention anything about her hair when I spoke to him."

"He wouldn't. He thought her hair looked just fine short. Pauline would have looked beautiful to him even if she'd been bald."

"Was there anything else bothering your sister prior to her death?"

"Nothing. Pauline was always happy. She honestly was."

"Can you think of anyone who might have wanted to hurt her?"

"No one. Everyone loved her. She was that kind of

person."

Janet Wesley spent the next hour sharing memories of her sister. Several times, she broke down and cried. There had obviously been a strong bond between the siblings just as there was between me and Kathy.

I was getting nowhere fast, and had next to nothing to go on. I had to find out what the police knew. The crime scene reports might throw more light on the murders, and there was always the possibility that the police had deliberately held back some information from the press. On a long shot, and with little expectation, I called Jack Maxwell who was his usual, charming self. He refused point blank to see me, and told me to stay out of his investigation.

Like *that* was going to happen.

I had some time before my appointment with Trisha Lamb's brother, so I decided to go back to my flat and practise a few spells. I half expected to find my mother hovering about the place, but there was no sign of her. She was probably still exhausted from our session earlier. Much as I liked the idea of having her around, I was pleased to be able to practise spells without anyone looking over my shoulder. I'd never been a good pupil; I'd always found it easier to learn alone.

The spell that caught my eye was called 'power', which according to the description, would make me twenty times stronger than normal. The spell would only last for five minutes. I'd noticed a lot of the spells were only effective for a short period of time.

My biggest problem was the speed at which I was able to

cast the spells. Under normal circumstances, it wouldn't be an issue, but if I was in imminent danger, I'd need to be much faster or I might end up on the wrong side of dead.

I put the book of spells onto the breakfast bar, and began to picture the images: dolphin, mountain stream, snowdrops, antelopes, storm clouds, and so the list went on.

It took me almost ninety seconds. Fat lot of good that would be if I was in a tight spot. Had it even worked? I didn't feel any different. There was only one way to find out. I grabbed one leg of the sofa and lifted. It felt as light as a feather. With practically no effort, I hoisted it above my head.

"Wow!"

I needed something heavier to really test my strength. I opened the French doors, being careful not to break them, and walked out into the garden. After a quick check that there was no one at the windows on the upper floor, I grabbed hold of the ornamental bird bath. I'd bought it the previous summer, so I could sit and watch the birds drink and bathe—another reason why I didn't want to bring Winky home. It was cast from concrete and weighed a ton. It had taken two burly men to carry it from their truck, and even they had struggled. I took a deep breath, bent my legs and—

"Wow!" It was so easy. I was holding it above my head, and yet it felt no heavier than a loaf of bread. Dare I take one hand away? Why not? I dropped one arm to my side, and held the bird bath with only one hand. This was fantastic—

"Oh bum!" I ducked to one side as the bird bath crashed

to the ground and shattered into a thousand pieces. What an idiot. I'd totally forgotten the spell only lasted for five minutes. One moment it had felt as light as a feather, the next it had been like trying to balance an elephant on my hand. What a mess! It had cost a small fortune too.

Just a minute! I had an idea. After a quick check in the book to remind myself of the images I needed, I cast the 'take it back' spell. Seconds later, the bird bath had been restored to its former glory. I was beginning to like being a witch.

Talk about a kid in a sweet shop. Now I'd got over my self-doubt, I couldn't wait to try out more spells. I decided the best approach would be to focus on memorising the spells that I'd already tested before I moved on to the others.

I was just beginning to think there was no one in, when the door cracked open.

"What?" The man sounded half asleep.

"Derek Cairn?"

"Who are you?"

"Jill Gooder. I called you yesterday. Remember?"

"Just a minute." He closed the door in my face, and left me standing in the corridor. The block of flats was run-down and in urgent need of a coat of paint, and air fresheners.

I was about to knock again when the door opened.

"Come in." He was wearing a crumpled, long sleeved tee-shirt and baggy tracksuit bottoms. "Sorry about the mess."

Not as sorry as I was. The living room wasn't fit for

purpose—nothing could have survived there. There were half eaten takeaways, still in their boxes, on every surface. Beer cans and wine bottles, most of them empty, littered the floor. I'd thought Mrs V's obsession with collecting yarn was bad enough, but this guy seemed to collect scissors. They were all over the place. Not at all freaky.

"Grab a seat," he said, as he sat back on what, underneath all the debris, was probably a sofa.

"I'm okay, thanks."

"You a private eye?"

"Investigator." I hated the label 'private eye'. "Harry Lamb tells me that your sister visited you regularly."

"I don't know why she married that ass. She could have done much better for herself. I told her so."

The smell of alcohol in the room was overpowering. On a shelf on the far wall was a framed photograph, which I recognised as Trisha Lamb. She was arm in arm with a handsome young man—both of them smiling. Happier days. Next to the photograph were two small trophies. If this room was anything to go by, they hadn't been awarded by 'Homes and Gardens'.

"How did she seem the last time you saw her?" I said.

"She was upset because she didn't know how he'd take it."

"How *who* would take *what*?"

"Harry, who do you think? She was going to tell him it was over between them. Took her long enough." His words were slurred. I couldn't be sure if he was upset at talking about his sister or if it was the alcohol taking its toll.

"Are you sure that's what she was going to do?"

"Course I'm sure. She was my sister. My big sister. We told each other everything."

"Are you seriously suggesting that your sister was murdered by her husband?"

"Who else?"

"The Bugle seems to think there may be a serial killer at large, and that your sister was killed because of her name."

"Trisha?"

"No, her surname—Lamb. There have been two other murders where the victims have had an 'animal' surname: Lyon and Fox. They're calling him the 'Animal'."

"I don't read the news. I still think Harry did it. He wants locking up or better still, stringing up."

Even as he was talking to me, I could see Cairn's eyelids starting to close. Maybe he was on something stronger than just alcohol.

Back outside, I sucked in the fresh air. After that experience, I'd need to fumigate my clothes. I prided myself on being a good judge of character, and I'd pegged Harry Lamb as a loving husband. Could I have got it wrong? If there was even a hint of truth in what Derek Cairn had said, I might have to take another look at Mr Lamb.

Chapter 14

The next morning, I was able to recall all of the spells that I'd tried to commit to memory the previous day. Result!

I planned to get to the police station at around ten o'clock because I figured they would have completed their morning briefings by then. I considered calling in at the office first, but I couldn't face the Mrs V and Winky show. Instead, as it was such a beautiful morning, I took a walk through the local park, which was always quiet at that time of day.

A middle-aged man out for a jog bid me 'good morning' as he passed by. I waited until he was about a hundred yards ahead, and then cast the 'faster' spell. As soon as I took the first step, the spell kicked in and I shot past the jogger so quickly he didn't even see me. When I reached the gates, I waited. A few seconds later he appeared.

"Morning," I said.

"Morning?" The look on his face was priceless. I felt a little guilty for having used the spell for such a trivial thing. Maybe there was some kind of witch's code that stated that magic should only be used for good and worthy causes. Hopefully not. I didn't want to get a reputation as a bad witch.

Just as I'd hoped, the car park at the police station was almost empty. My biggest concern was the time factor. Once I'd cast the 'invisible' spell, I'd have only ten minutes. Any longer than that, and I'd have some explaining to do. I ignored the public entrance at the front of the building. Instead, I made my way around the back and waited near to the large metal barrier. This entrance was used by official police vehicles. Because time was at a premium, I didn't want to cast the spell a second sooner than I had to. I watched the traffic until I saw what I was waiting for. A patrol car was indicating to turn into the police station. I cast the spell or at least I hoped I had. Had it worked? I could still see myself, but I knew that was always the case. When the police car came to a halt at the barrier, I stepped forward to check if I could see my reflection in the side window. Result! Hey, I was getting good at this witch stuff. I followed the car into the car park, and waited for the officers to make their way inside the building. When one of them punched the four digit code into the lock, I memorised the keys — the combination might come in handy in the future. The door was on a powerful spring and I had to be quick to sneak inside with them before it sprang closed.

There was no time to lose. Although I'd been to the police station before, I'd never been further than the interview rooms. I took the first flight of stairs I came to, and then made my way along the corridor. Three doors in, I hit pay dirt. The sign on the door read 'Jack Maxwell'. Was he in? I knocked. There was no reply and no movement inside. I made sure the corridor was clear, and then tried the handle. Bingo! The door wasn't locked. This was going far better than I could have hoped.

Whoops! Spoke too soon. I'd only taken a few steps into his office when I heard the door handle turn behind me. My instinct was to dive for cover, but then I remembered there was no need. I was invisible.

"Is someone following up on that?" Jack Maxwell said.
"Yes, sir." The second man was taller, and several years younger than Maxwell. "Mike Jones is on his way over to see him now."
"What do you reckon?" Maxwell asked.
"I don't know. I thought we'd dismissed the 'animal' connection, sir?"
"Let's see what Mike comes up with."
Maxwell turned around and was now facing me. Even though I knew he couldn't see me, it was still incredibly unnerving. I checked my watch. I still had another six minutes of invisibility.
"Where's the meeting?" Maxwell was so close now that I could have reached out and stroked his face. What? I only said that to illustrate how close he was—not because I actually wanted to stroke his face. Sheesh! I hated the man, remember?
"Incident room three, sir."
"Okay. Let's get up there."
On a hunch, I followed the two men out of the room and up one flight of stairs. The rooms on this floor were much larger and had windows that looked out onto a central corridor. The two men entered incident room three—I followed. On the back wall, was a huge whiteboard with 'Lyon/Lamb/Fox?' written across the top. I took the '?' after Caroline Fox's name to indicate the uncertainty as to whether or not the third murder was related to the first two. Below the names were a number of photographs—none of them made easy viewing. It was obvious from these that Mrs Lyon and Mrs Lamb had both died from multiple stab wounds to their upper body. The third victim, my client's girlfriend,

had been strangled – there was clear bruising to the neck.

I was running out of time. If the spell ran out while I was still in the incident room, I'd be arrested and Maxwell would throw the book at me, but I couldn't leave until I had all the information I needed.

Ninety seconds left. Come on! Think! I needed somewhere to hide until I could use the 'invisible' spell again. But where? There was a cupboard over to my left, but how was I supposed to get into it unnoticed? I had little faith in the police, but even they would notice a door opening by itself.

One minute left! How was I going to explain my presence? More to the point – how was I going to explain appearing out of thin air? I wasn't sure which laws I'd broken, but you could bet your life Jack Maxwell would know, and he'd take great pleasure in locking me up, and throwing away the key.

Thirty seconds left! The room was set out in a classroom style with rows of tables that faced a long desk at the front. I hurried to the front, and ducked underneath the desk.

There was just enough room for me to squeeze in – I had my knees clamped tight against my chest.

Ten, nine, eight, seven, six, five, four, three, two, one. The spell had run its course and I was visible again. It felt as though my heart was about to burst out of my chest. I waited – half-expecting someone to say 'who's that under the desk', but no one did – the modesty board had saved me.

Jack Maxwell, who was standing at the front of the room,

to the left of the desk, began to address the members of his team.

"Okay. A quick recap for the benefit of those who have just joined this case. The first victim was Mrs Pauline Lyon—husband—Geoffrey Lyon. She died from multiple stab wounds inflicted by a thin bladed instrument. The second victim was Trisha Lamb—husband—Harry Lamb. She also died from multiple stab wounds which were inflicted by a similar weapon. We believe that the same man may have been responsible for both of these murders."

He moved towards the centre of the whiteboard and was now standing directly in front of the desk; a mere two feet from where I was hiding. I pushed myself further back into the space trying to make my body as small as possible.

That's when I spotted them.

Jack Maxwell, the tough, arrogant asshat of a detective was wearing Tweety Pie socks. I clamped my hand tight over my mouth. If I laughed I'd be a dead woman.

"This is Caroline Fox," he continued. "So far there is nothing to connect her murder to the other two. The cause of death was strangulation. The press and others have been trying to push the notion of a serial killer because of the women's surnames, but so far there's nothing to link this third murder. However, we're keeping an open mind."

For the next ten minutes, the detectives who had been on the case for some time ran through what they had done so far. If they were throwing this much manpower at the investigation, they must have been under considerable pressure to make an arrest. I listened to what everyone had to say. The bottom line seemed to be that, so far, they had drawn a blank. They obviously had no idea who was behind any of the murders — serial killer or not. Maxwell stepped forward, so he was right next to the desk. His socks looked even more hilarious close to.

Oh no! Why had my body chosen now to betray me? The toes on my right foot were beginning to cramp. I tried wiggling them, but that only seemed to make it worse. I needed to stand up, so I could get the blood circulating again, but if I did that I'd be the one who'd be out of circulation, for a very long time. Banged up in prison.

Luckily, the cramp passed after a few seconds. Maybe I was going to get away with this after all. Another five minutes, and I'd be able to cast the spell again.

"Okay? Anyone have any questions?" Maxwell asked, as he disappeared to my left.

It took a few seconds for me to realise what the noise was, and then I saw the chair. He was wheeling it towards the desk. I was done for. As soon as he sat at the desk his feet would touch me. What would I say? I was pretty good at talking my way out of awkward situations, but this? The chair was opposite the desk now. Any moment now he'd sit down. I was as good as dead.

The door opened.

"Sir, I think you'll want to see this," a male voice said.

"Okay everyone. We'll call this a wrap and convene again tomorrow at nine a.m. unless anything significant comes up before then."

The room filled with the sound of chairs being pushed under tables. Maxwell moved out of my field of vision, and I heard him say. "Let's take this down to my office,

Mike."

I stayed where I was until I was able to cast the spell again. Once invisible, I crawled out from under the desk; my legs felt like jelly. The incident room was deserted, so I spent as long as I dared reading through the notes on the whiteboard. A few snippets of information caught my eye:

- The description of the suspect had been provided by a neighbour. A seventy year old woman who, according to the notes, had fading eye sight.
- As well as bruising to the neck, Caroline Fox had bruising and cuts on one of her fingers. She also had a small, circular puncture mark just below her left ear.
- Danny Peterson had been at his brother's house when Caroline Fox was murdered. I assumed it was this alibi that had eliminated him as a suspect.

Once I was sure the corridor outside was clear, I left the incident room and retraced my steps down to the ground floor. Time was running out. I had to make my escape quickly or I'd be in deep doo-doo. It was too risky to leave the same way as I'd come in, because if the spell wore off before I got through the barrier, I'd be spotted for sure.

I headed for the front desk where two police officers were on duty. One officer was attending to a rather noisy middle-aged woman who wanted to know if he was going to find her 'Alfie'. Who Alfie was, I had no idea. And, judging by the expression on the officer's face, he didn't much care. The other officer was talking to a young woman who'd had her handbag 'nicked'. There was just enough room for me to squeeze between the two officers, but I had to be careful when I jumped off the counter, so that I didn't collide with those queuing to be seen.

As I reached the outer door, I saw my reflection in the glass. The spell had worn off again.

"What are you doing here?" Jack Maxwell's voice froze me to the spot. I turned around to find him standing behind the counter. Had he seen me appear out of thin air?

"I came to see you," I said with all the confidence I could muster.

"I told you on the phone that I have nothing to say to you."

Everyone was staring at me.

"I only need a few minutes of your time." I moved closer to the counter, and was now wedged between the middle-aged woman looking for Alfie, and the young woman who'd had her handbag stolen.

"Do you have any new information relating to the case?" Maxwell asked.

"No, but—"

"Then you're wasting my time," he said, before disappearing into the back.

I shrugged, and started back to the door.

"Don't worry, love," an old man wearing a flat cap said, as I walked by him. "Useless this lot. All of them."

That was a close call. Maxwell had seen me by the door and must have assumed I was on my way into the building. His attitude was really starting to annoy me now—who did he think he was? A little co-operation wouldn't hurt anyone. And what was with those socks?

Chapter 15

What crisis would be waiting for me at the office this time? It was only a matter of time before Mrs V strangled Winky with one of her scarves. What a pair. Mrs V I'd inherited from my dad, but Winky — I had only myself to blame for him.

I took a short-cut through the alleyway between the supermarket and the cinema. It was a route I often took during daylight hours. Midway along the alley, I began to regret my decision. A thick fog descended from nowhere, and I was struggling to see the ground in front of me. I'm not usually the nervous type, but this freaked me out. It wasn't just the lack of visibility; something else didn't feel right. It was the silence — an unnatural silence. The alleyway ran between two busy streets, and yet I couldn't hear any voices or traffic.

I *could* hear footsteps though. Someone, maybe more than one person, was coming my way. I stood perfectly still — waiting. The footsteps grew louder. I strained my eyes trying to see something. Anything.

The hooded figure, dressed in a grey cloak, stood at least seven feet tall. The hood hung low over his face so I could see no more than a chiselled chin. More footsteps — behind me this time. I spun around to see another hooded figure. I was trapped. I instinctively knew these must be the 'Followers' that Aunt Lucy and my mother had warned me about.

I edged back until I was leaning against the supermarket wall. I had to focus. My first thought was to use the 'invisible' spell, but it was less than thirty minutes since I'd used it last. I wasn't convinced the 'faster' or 'power' spells would be any good against these adversaries. My one hope was the 'lightning bolt.' I had to get this right first time if I was going to see off both of them.

The Follower on my right was closest to me. I cast the spell and pointed my finger at his chest. The force of the lightning bolt still took me by surprise. He let out an ear-piercing scream as he imploded before my eyes. I turned quickly to face my other assailant, but I was too slow. He was only a few feet away, and would be on me before I had time to cast the spell. Pity. I was beginning to enjoy being a witch. I closed my eyes and tried not to think about whatever ghastly fate was about to befall me.

The scream sounded as though it had come from the depths of hell. I opened my eyes just in time to see the second Follower implode. No sooner had he disappeared than the fog lifted, and the sounds of voices and traffic from the nearby streets returned.

"Are you okay?" Aunt Lucy took my hand.

"Thank you." I sighed. "I thought I was a goner."

"Don't mention it, my dear. You did really well. You had no chance of taking them both out."

"How did you know I was in danger?"

"Your mother gave me the nod. She thought you might need a hand. It's hard for her to have to look on without being able to help."

"How did you manage to get here so quickly?"

"I'm a witch, dear." She smiled. "I have my methods."

"Thank you again."

"No problem. I really do hope you'll come to Candlefield again soon. Your cousins and grandma can't wait to meet you."

"I will. I promise." I took her hand. "I'm sorry I didn't believe you before."
"Don't give it another thought. This must all have come as quite a shock."
"It has, but I shouldn't have been so horrible to you."
"Just you take care. I doubt you have seen the last of the Followers."

I loved my niece and nephew to bits, but I found them really hard work. How Kathy managed to be with them twenty-four seven was beyond me. What is it with kids? They're relentless. I'm sure I was never like that. When I was a kid, I liked to read, and to play with my beanies. I'd never felt the need to run around the house screaming at the top of my voice. That had been more Kathy's thing, I seem to recall.
I'd tried to talk my way out of the party, but Kathy had seen straight through my feeble excuses and threatened to disown me if I didn't turn up or tried to slip away early. She never let me forget that she was the older sister. She was a bossy cow, but I loved her anyway.
I'd wanted to buy a book for Lizzie, but Kathy had insisted I buy her Lego.
"More Lego?"
"She wants the Lego Fire Station."
"Couldn't she make a fire station out of the Lego she already has? I thought that was the whole idea. What about a chemistry set?"
"She's five, Jill. What would she want with a chemistry set?"
"I had one when I was her age."
"Yeah, but you were a weird kid."

"I wasn't weird!"

"You used to catalogue your beanies. That's weird."

I ignored the jibe. "Are you sure she wouldn't like a few beanies?"

"She wants a Lego Fire Station. Besides, if she wants to play with beanies, she can always borrow yours."

"I don't have any beanies now."

"I've seen them. In your wardrobe."

"Okay, okay. I'll get her the Lego Fire Station."

How did Kathy know about my beanies? She must have been nosing around my flat. Borrow *my* beanies? *Lizzie*? No way! They wouldn't last five minutes. I'd have to find somewhere safe to keep them away from Kathy's prying eyes. I could tell her that I'd sold them.

"Auntie Jill!" Lizzie came running across the room. "What have you bought me?"

"Lizzie!" Kathy scolded gently. "Let your auntie get in the door first."

"What is it, Auntie Jill?" Lizzie looked up at the present that I was holding.

"It's a chemistry set."

Lizzie's face fell.

"It's a *what?*" Kathy shot me her familiar death-stare.

"Kidding. I'm only kidding." I deposited the present into her Lizzie's tiny hands, and watched in disbelief at the speed with which she ripped off the paper that I'd spent the best part of twenty minutes wrapping it in.

"Lego Fire Station!" Lizzie screamed with delight, as she pulled open the lid.

"Say thank you to Auntie Jill." Kathy flashed me a smile.

"Thanks, Auntie Jill," Lizzie said. She was already

beginning to assemble the fire station.

The meal was pandemonium. Ten kids—two for each year of Lizzie's age—sat around a table meant to seat six. Kathy, Peter and me acted as waiters, cleaners and referees while the children screamed and squabbled their way through a mountain of sandwiches, jelly, ice cream, and birthday cake. Kathy somehow managed to avoid all-out war when one of the kids took it upon himself to blow out the candles before Lizzie had the chance to do it. Once the meal was over, Peter stayed in the living room and began to organise party games while Kathy and I escaped to the kitchen.

"Will Peter be okay in there by himself?" I felt a little guilty at leaving him at the mercy of ten rampaging kids.

"Are you kidding? He loves all those games. He's still a big kid at heart."

"I'll wash, you can dry," I said. The mountain of pots on the drainer was threatening to topple onto the floor.

"The dishes can wait." Kathy opened the fridge. "We're having a glass of wine. We've earned it."

"Cheers!" I joined Kathy at the kitchen table. "How much longer will the party go on for?"

"Don't worry. The parents will be here in another hour to pick up their little darlings."

"I'm glad I came."

"Liar!" Kathy laughed. "You had me going for a minute there with the chemistry set."

"I still think it would have been a better present."

Kathy downed the wine, and poured herself another. "Top-up?"

"No thanks."

The noise from the next room was unbelievable — even with the door closed.

"They're playing pass the parcel," Kathy said.

"How can you tell?"

"When you've been to as many birthday parties as I have, you get to know. Anyway, enough of the kids. I need some grown-up conversation. What's happening with the murder case?"

"Not much so far. The police may be coming around to the idea of a serial killer."

"Did Jack Maxwell tell you that?"

"Are you kidding? He won't even give me the time of day. Arrogant sod."

"So how do you know?"

"I have my sources."

The door flew open, and a red-faced Peter said, "Where's the donkey?"

"Under the sideboard," Kathy said.

"Donkey?" I asked, once Peter had closed the door.

"'Pin the tail on the donkey.' Don't you remember anything about kids' parties?"

I shrugged. I remembered that I hated them — especially the games. Mum and Dad had given us the choice of a day out or a party for our birthdays. I'd always gone for the day out, but Kathy had always had a party. And she'd always forced me to be there.

"Have you heard any more from your new family?" Kathy was once again topping up her glass. Now I knew her secret for getting through the party.

"No, nothing." I was hardly going to tell her that I'd had a conversation with my mother's ghost or that Aunt Lucy had saved me from the Followers. And I certainly couldn't tell her that I was a witch with magical powers. Not unless I wanted her to have me committed.

Kathy gave me that look. The one she always gave me when she knew I was lying. Luckily, before she had a chance to call me on it, the door flew open again.

"Auntie Jill," Lizzie screamed. "Come and look."

She grabbed my hand, and led me through to the next room where Peter was trying to separate two boys who seemed to be having a dispute over a pirate's hat.

"Why aren't you playing the party games?" I asked Lizzie as she dragged me towards her bedroom.

"I don't like blind man's buff. It's scary," she said almost matter-of-factly. "Look!" She pulled me into her bedroom. There on the floor was the fire station, now fully assembled.

"That's great. It didn't take you long to put it together."

She smiled — her face full of pride. "It was easy."

"Wow!" I caught sight of a huge Lego hotel on the dressing table. "Did you make that too?"

"No, silly." She laughed. "Daddy made that one. It took him ages and ages."

I'd no idea that it was possible to create such an elaborate building from Lego. It was enormous.

"Your daddy is very clever. Can I take a closer look?"

"You have to be careful," she warned.

I nodded, and began to walk across the room.

Now in my own defence, I should say that the room was dimly lit. The only light came from a small bedside lamp. Plus, the fire-engine was the same red as the carpet, so I didn't spot it until I'd stepped on it. Once I'd lost my footing, my survival instincts kicked in. Naturally, I put my arms out in an attempt to stop my fall.

"No!" Lizzie screamed. "You broke it!"

I'd managed to break my fall, but in the process had knocked the hotel off the dressing table. It was now in a million pieces on the floor.

"Lizzie, wait!" I called after her, but she'd already fled the scene of devastation. "Daddy! Mummy! Auntie Jill has broken my hotel!"

Now I was really in for it. Peter would kill me — it must have taken him days to build it.

"What's wrong, poppet?" Peter said.

"What's going on?" Kathy sounded concerned.

Concentrate. I had to concentrate.

"Jill?" Kathy pushed open the door. "What's — ?" She stared past me at the dressing table.

I flashed my best, nonchalant smile.

Lizzie, her eyes red, appeared at her mum's side. Peter was standing behind the two of them.

"I thought you said it was broken?" Kathy crouched down next to her daughter.

"It was, Mummy. She broke it."

"It looks okay to me, poppet." Peter put a hand on his daughter's head.

"I tripped on the fire engine." I pointed to the toy. "But I managed to catch myself. Lizzie must have thought I was going to knock the hotel over." I smiled at Lizzie. She didn't smile back. Instead, she eyed me suspiciously.

Chapter 16

"Thanks for coming Jill," Kathy said when I was ready to leave. The kids had all been collected by their parents and Peter was putting Lizzie and Mikey to bed.

"No problem. I enjoyed it."

"Liar." Kathy grinned.

"I'll call you."

As I made my way to the car, I looked back at the house, and saw a little face at one of the windows. What kind of aunt was I? My poor niece would probably have nightmares because of me. But what was I supposed to do? Tell them I'd used a 'take it back' spell? Lizzie was looking at me like I was some kind of witch.

I'd had my phone switched off during the party—Kathy had insisted. She'd said she didn't trust me, and even suggested I might have arranged for Mrs V to call and say I was needed on urgent business. As if I would have stooped so low. Sure enough, when I switched it back on, there were nine missed calls. The log showed they were all from my office. I'd told Mrs V to call me thirty minutes after the party started to get me out of there. Seven of the calls were within a few minutes of each other, but the last two were only a few minutes ago.

I called the office. "Mrs V?"

"Where were you?" She sounded annoyed. Had Winky managed to open the linen basket?

"Kathy made me switch my phone off. What's up?" I knew something must have happened because normally Mrs V would have left the office by now.

"Have you seen the news?"

"No. Why?"

"There's been an arrest in the Fox case."

"What? Okay, thanks. I'll take a look. You can get off home now. Thanks for staying."

I fired up the news app on my phone and checked the local stories. Sure enough the main headline was 'Serial killer arrested'.

The story was obviously still developing, so there were practically no details other than the fact that an arrest had been made. I doubted the police would have used the term 'serial killer'. That was more likely to have come from the news desk. A man had been arrested, but it wasn't clear if he had been charged with one or all of the murders.

My phone rang.

"Have you seen it?" Danny Peterson said.

"Yes. Have the police been in touch with you?"

"No. I rang them but they won't tell me anything. Is it Caroline's killer?"

"I don't know, Danny. Leave it with me and I'll see what I can find out. I'll call you as soon as I know anything."

I called the police station and used the name of one of my press contacts rather than my own.

"There's a press conference scheduled for nine-thirty in the morning," the bored voice said.

"Can you tell me if the suspect has been charged with all three murders?"

"There's a press conference scheduled for nine-thirty in the morning."

I wasn't going to get anything out of him. I was tempted to pay another *invisible* visit to the police station, but that seemed unnecessarily risky. For once in my life, I'd have to be patient and see what the morning press conference revealed.

Back at the flat, I was still feeling a tinge of guilt over the Lego hotel incident. I could still see the look on Lizzie's face. To take my mind off it, I decided to practise and memorise some more spells. I was slowly building up quite an arsenal of them. It was all still very exciting, but would have been even better if I could have shared it with someone. I'd have loved to shown off my 'powers' to Kathy. Her face would have been a picture.

I came across one spell which looked particularly fascinating. As soon as I spotted the 'mind read' spell, I knew it was one I wanted to master. As its name suggested, it would allow me to read another person's thoughts. As always, the spell came with all kinds of conditions and restrictions. It wouldn't work on sups or on any human under the age of eighteen. And, it would only work on someone standing directly in front of me — I had to be looking them in the eye. It lasted for only thirty seconds, which didn't sound like very long. The worst restriction of all was that I could only use that spell once a year. Who knew magic came with so much red tape?

The next morning, it was raining and blowing a gale. The press conference had been scheduled for nine-thirty, and I'd arrived at police HQ fifteen minutes early. I needn't have bothered because a notice on the door said the press conference had been put back to ten o'clock. There was a huge crowd of reporters and TV crews — not surprising — this was Washbridge's first serial killer. I wasn't sure if I'd get inside because I didn't have any press credentials. I planned on walking in with one of the TV crews—I doubted they'd bother checking everyone. If that didn't work, I had other less conventional options open to me.

"Have they caught the 'Animal'?" a voice to my right said.

The man was wearing a press badge, and I could see he was from the Bugle. His question didn't appear to be directed at anyone in particular.

"No idea, Jimmy." The reply came from a young woman, who was holding a microphone. "They're keeping tight-lipped on this one."

The doors opened, and the crowd poured inside. As I'd hoped, no one asked for my ID. The small conference room was full to bursting, but I managed to manoeuvre my way towards the front. Once the doors had been closed behind us, Jack Maxwell, flanked by two other plain clothes officers, appeared through a door to our right. Even before he could speak, numerous voices hurled questions his way. Inscrutable as ever, he stood in silence at the front of the room—waiting.

Only when the room fell silent again, did he speak, "Yesterday, at four-fifteen Martin Kilburn was arrested and charged with the murders of Pauline Lyon, Trisha Lamb and Caroline Fox. He'll appear in court this afternoon."

"So, Kilburn is the 'Animal'?" A male voice came from somewhere behind me.

"I'm not sure I understand the question," Maxwell answered—deadpan.

"Was the murderer known to the victims?"

"It doesn't appear so."

"Is Kilburn local?"

"Yes."

"I thought you said that Caroline Fox's murder had a different MO from the first two murders?" I shouted above the other voices.

Maxwell's gaze met mine. I wondered for a moment if he'd have me thrown out because he knew I wasn't press. "That's correct. The MO for Caroline Fox's murder was different."

"But you've charged Kilburn with all three murders," I pressed.

"That's what I said."

Shortly afterwards, Maxwell called an end to the press conference, and cleared the room. I was almost out of the door when I felt a hand on my shoulder.

"Can I have a word?" Maxwell said. It wasn't a question. He waited until the last of the reporters left, and then got in my face, "Since when are you press?"

I shrugged. If he expected an apology, he was going to be disappointed.

"The next time you gatecrash a press conference, I'll have you arrested."

I laughed. "And charged with what, exactly?"

"Obstructing the police."

"Grow up. Don't you have anything better to worry about than me?"

"You've been warned." He turned and began to walk away.

"Wait!"

"What now?" He turned back to face me. This was my opportunity. I cast the 'mind read' spell.

"How did you identify and capture the suspect?" I

asked.

I knew he wouldn't answer, but I was playing a hunch. If my question stimulated his mind to run through the events leading to the arrest, I'd be able to read his thoughts.

"It's time for you to leave." He took hold of my arm. As he did, the spell began to work. I could read his thoughts as clearly as if he'd spoken them.

It wasn't what I'd been expecting.

Danny Peterson was waiting for me back at the office. Winky was perched on the window sill, glaring at the young man.

"Is that old lady okay?" Danny said.

"Who, Mrs V? Yeah, she's fine — mostly."

"She asked me if I wanted a scarf. Or a cat."

"Take no notice."

"I just came by to say thanks."

"There's nothing to thank me for. I didn't really make any headway with your case."

"You managed to get them to see it was the work of a serial killer."

"Not really. Detective Maxwell must have worked that out all by himself. I'm the last person on earth that he'd listen to."

"I don't trust this guy," Winky said, still glaring at Danny.

"Hush!" I said to Winky.

"Sorry?" Danny looked confused.

"His eyes are too close together," Winky hissed.

"Quiet."

Danny looked really confused now — little wonder.

"Not you. I was talking to the cat."

"Oh." Danny gave me a sympathetic smile.

"Do you know the man they've arrested?" I asked.

Danny shook his head. "I've never heard of him, but I hope they lock him up and throw away the key."

I waited until I heard the outer door close, and then turned on Winky. "Don't do that!"

"What?"

"Talk to me when I'm with someone."

"Why not?"

"Because—because you're a cat."

"So?"

"It's off-putting."

"I still don't trust him. Did you see his eyes? Untrustworthy."

"You're hardly in a position to judge someone based upon their eyes." I turned away, and said under my breath, "Or lack of them."

"I heard that!"

Aunt Lucy was thrilled when I called to say I was going to pay her a visit. I hadn't planned on going to Candlefield so soon, but now that the Fox case was wrapped up, there wasn't really anything to stop me. I wanted to practise my magic in the open, and I assumed there would be more opportunity to do that among my own kind. *My own kind?* Listen to me. It still felt weird to think of myself as a sup.

The road sign and turn-off were exactly where they should have been. I still couldn't get my head around the idea that humans couldn't see either of them. I was really excited about meeting my cousins and grandma. Maybe they'd give me some pointers to improve my spell-casting technique. I was definitely getting better—way faster than my early attempts. When I'd spoken to Aunt Lucy on the phone, I'd asked her for her address and directions. Cryptically, she'd said, "Don't worry your head about those, dear. The car will find us."

I'd been a little dubious, but as soon as I arrived in Candlefield, the car did indeed seem to know where it was going. It was as though I had an invisible SatNav, which was guiding me to my destination. The cottage was unmistakeably Aunt Lucy's. Every surface was painted a different pastel colour.

"Hi, Jill!" She appeared in the doorway.

"Where shall I park the car?"

"It'll be fine right there. Do you have bags?"

"Just this." I pulled the small case out of the back seat.

"Give me a hug!" She threw her arms around me. "Come inside. I was about to make a pot of tea."

Never in my entire life had I seen such a colourful cupcake. "That was delicious," I said, a little guilty at the speed at which I'd devoured it.

"You have the twins to thank for that. Did I tell you they have a cake-shop and tea room?"

"They must do very well if this is anything to go by."

"You'll have to pay it a visit while you're here."

"I'd like that. I'm looking forward to meeting them."

"I've arranged for them and Grandma to come over this evening. They're all really excited about meeting you." She hesitated. "Well, the twins are. Grandma doesn't really do excited."

"Will I have time to take a look around the village first?"

"Of course, my dear. Dinner is at six."

I checked my watch; it had just turned three. "I don't expect it will take long to see everything."

"You might be surprised." There was a mischievous glint in her eye.

"What?"

"Candlefield isn't like anywhere you've been before. Not everything is what it appears to be, including the size of the village."

A few weeks earlier, I might have taken her comment with a pinch of salt, but after my experience with the disappearing road, I was no longer so dismissive. "I'll see you later then." I turned to walk away, but then hesitated. "Should I worry about the Dark One and his cronies?"

"You should be safe during daylight hours, but it might be best if you don't venture out alone after dark until you know the lie of the land. It's certainly much safer for you to be here than in the human world."

"Okay, thanks. See you later then."

Chapter 17

I'd been walking up the same winding road for almost ten minutes, and I still hadn't reached the top of the hill. From Aunt Lucy's house, the hill had looked no more than a couple of minutes' climb. But then, Aunt Lucy had warned me that not everything was what it appeared to be in Candlefield.

Every house I passed seemed to be unique unlike the identikit houses I was used to seeing in Washbridge. I was fascinated by the different shapes, sizes and colours of the properties that bordered the road. Every time I spotted someone at a window, they greeted me with a smile and a wave. Back home, I'd have been given a dirty look or worse.

When I finally made it to the top of the hill, the view took my breath away. Until then, I'd thought of Candlefield as a village, but it was the size of a large city which stretched as far as the eye could see. How could somewhere like this exist, and yet be invisible to humans?

No wonder Aunt Lucy had been amused when I'd said it wouldn't take long to look around the place. It would have taken me at least a week. It was like no other city I'd ever seen. There were no skyscrapers; the tallest building I could see was no more than three stories high. From my vantage point, I could see several parks and two lakes; one much larger than the other. To my right, was what appeared to be a large open-air market. To my left, in the distance, was some kind of amusement park.

I didn't know where to begin. It would probably have been better to wait until Aunt Lucy could show me around, but I'd come this far, and I wasn't about to turn back. I'd need to keep a check on the time though to make sure I wasn't late getting back.

I've always loved markets, so I made my way there. The normal laws of time and distance didn't seem to apply in Candlefield. From the top of the hill, the market had looked to be at least a fifteen minute walk away, but within no more than a minute I was there.

It felt as though the whole population of Candlefield was at the market. The space between the rows of stalls was narrow, and at times I felt as though I was being carried along by the crowd. Were all these people sups? I supposed they must be because humans couldn't visit Candlefield. I found myself staring at people. Was he a werewolf? Was she a witch or perhaps a vampire? Should I be able to tell? Did they know I was a witch? They all looked — err — human, I guess. If I'd met any of them on the street in Washbridge, I wouldn't have given them a second glance.

It was only when I came upon a stall selling soft drinks that I realised how thirsty I was. There were dozens of flavours, none of which I'd ever heard of: zutaberry, quilberry and many others. The woman behind the counter must have noticed my puzzled expression because she called to me.

"Can I help you?"

I waved my credit card at her. "I don't imagine you take these?" I was so used to using plastic that I carried very little cash.

She smiled. "You won't be able to use that anywhere in Candlefield."

"Oh. Right. How much are the drinks?" I pulled out a

handful of coins from my pocket.

"Don't worry about it. Your Aunt Lucy said to put it on her account."

"Really? How did she know I'd come to your stall?"

"There isn't much your Aunt Lucy doesn't know. What flavour would you like?"

I ran my gaze over row after row of bottles. "What would you recommend?"

"Zutaberry is my favourite. Would you like to try it?"

I nodded, even though I was a little unsure about the dark green colour. I needn't have worried. It was absolutely delicious and just what I needed to quench my thirst. Next, I bought a bag of mixed fudge from the stall opposite. If I did move to Candlefield, I'd be in danger of putting on some serious weight.

There were lots of fascinating stalls. It was a good thing that they didn't take plastic or I'd have done some real damage to my credit card bill. As soon as I saw the silk scarf, I knew Kathy would have loved it. Peter said she had a silk scarf addiction, and he was probably right. In the end though, I didn't buy it. It would have been unfair to take advantage of Aunt Lucy's generosity, and besides I wasn't sure if I'd be able to take goods out of Candlefield. I made a mental note to ask Aunt Lucy how that worked.

The majority of the stalls were similar to those that you would find in the human world: food, clothes, toys etc. However, there were others that most definitely would not have been found outside of Candlefield. One of the most popular ones was selling books, but not just any old books — spell books. I studied the crowd of people who were gathered around the stall.

"See anything you like, Jill?" the woman behind the stall said.

I couldn't decide if I found it comforting or unnerving that everyone seemed to know my name.

"No, thanks. I'm okay."

"Are you sure? Aunt Lucy said you could put it on her account."

"Thanks, but I don't think I'm ready for another book just yet."

"No problem. Maybe when you move up a level. We're here three times a week if you need anything."

I'd lost track of time. It was only when I noticed the lights on the stalls had come on that I realised it was starting to go dark. I checked my watch. Twenty to six. Where had the time gone? How would it look if I was late for dinner? My new family would not be impressed. The square was still busy, so it took a couple of minutes just to make my way to the edge of the market. If I traced my way around the edge of the square, I should eventually find the road I came in on.

After ten minutes, I still hadn't seen any buildings I recognised. I was going to be late for sure. As I considered which way I should try next, I spotted them in the distance. Two hooded figures were making their way towards me. Followers! I had to get out of there. I could worry about finding Aunt Lucy's house later. I took the first street I came to, and ran as fast as I could. A hundred yards along the street, I spotted a recessed doorway to my right. If the Followers saw the street was deserted, hopefully they'd carry on their search of the square. My heart was pounding as I leaned with my back against the door. In the distance I could hear the sounds of the market. I waited, hardly daring to breathe. I'd give it five minutes—long enough for them to pass by the bottom of the street, and then I'd make a run for it.

My heart sank as I heard footsteps. They were only faint, as if they were walking on tip-toe. I tried the door, but it was locked. I was trapped.

The footsteps were much closer now. It would only be a matter of seconds before they found me. Hold on! How stupid was I? I didn't have to battle it out with them—I could use the 'invisible' spell. Why hadn't I thought of that back in the square? I'd have to hurry though.

"Holy cupcakes!" a female voice screamed.

"Crumbs!" another female voice yelled.

"What the?" I shouted.

I'm not sure who jumped the most. Me or the two young women who were now standing in front of me.

"Cousin Jill?" the one on the left said. "We've been looking for you everywhere. I'm Pearl."

"And I'm Amber."

They removed their hoods to reveal striking ginger hair. At first I thought my eyes were playing tricks on me, and that I was seeing double, but then I realised they were identical twins. Under their short, grey cloaks, they wore matching blue polka dot dresses, and as far as I could tell, the only way to tell them apart was by the small beauty spot on Amber's left cheek.

I sighed with relief. "I thought you were Followers."

"Us?" Amber giggled.

"Followers?" Pearl giggled too.

"It was the hoods," I said, feeling more than a little foolish. "I'm sorry you had to come looking for me. I got lost."

"Mum thought you probably had. That's why she sent us to find you."

"I hope she isn't angry."

"Don't worry," Pearl said. "I think she was half-expecting you to get lost. Candlefield is a big place."

"So I'm beginning to realise."

"Come on," Amber said, turning back down the alley. "We'd better get going."

I walked alongside the twins. They couldn't have been much taller than five two, but their bee-hive hairstyles added another six inches to their height. How could I have mistaken them for Followers? I was cracking up.

"I like your hair," I said.

"Thank you," they replied in unison.

"We had it done especially for the party." Pearl beamed.

"Party?"

"Well, it's not exactly a party, but it feels like one. It's not every day we get to meet our long-lost cousin."

"Have you always known about me then?"

"Of course. Your mum talked about you all the time. She was always showing us photos of you."

"She had photos of me?"

"Hundreds. She spent as much time following you around as she spent in Candlefield."

I felt a lump in my throat, and I had to fight back the tears. All those years I thought I'd been abandoned, but my mother had been with me all of the time.

Chapter 18

"So you're Jill," Grandma said. "Well it's about time we got to meet you, young lady."

There's no kind way to say this, so I'll just put it out there. Grandma looked every bit like the wicked witches I'd seen in fairy tales. All she needed was the pointed hat, and she could have graced any Halloween party.

"Pleased to meet you," I said while trying not to stare at the large wart on the end of her nose.

"You have a lot of catching up to do," she said. "You've wasted way too long living among those humans."

"Mother!" Aunt Lucy gave Grandma a withering look. "That's enough. It's not Jill's fault that she didn't know she was a witch. You know that."

"A witch always knows she's a witch," Grandma insisted. "Have you started to practise your spells?"

"I have, but I still have a lot to learn."

"If you need any help, you can always call on me."

"Thanks." Never going to happen. I'd never liked scary movies. The prospect of being alone with Grandma was way more frightening.

"Go and sit down, everyone." Aunt Lucy ushered us through to the dining room. "Dinner is almost ready."

Grandma sat at the head of the table. The twins sat together on one side, and I sat opposite them. Aunt Lucy's place was set at the other end of the table.

"What's it like being a detective?" Amber asked.

"Have you shot anyone?" Pearl joined in.

"It's not as exciting as you might think. And no, I haven't shot anyone."

"What was your most exciting case?"

"Girls!" Grandma gave them a disapproving look. "That's enough 'human' talk at the dining table. Jill is a witch now, so she'll be giving up all of that silly detective stuff."

"Sorry?" I wasn't sure I'd heard her correctly.

"I said that you'll be giving up all that detective nonsense when you move to Candlefield."

This was news to me. "Just a minute—"

"Dinner's ready," Aunt Lucy interrupted. When she caught my eye, she subtly shook her head, which I took to mean that I shouldn't engage with Grandma. I didn't want to spoil my first ever meal with my new family, so I let it go, but there was no way I'd be giving up my job or moving to Candlefield.

Aunt Lucy had made a pie. It was probably the largest pie I'd ever seen, and certainly the most delicious. It came with all the trimmings. My plate was overflowing, and by the time the meal was over, I was stuffed.

"Thank you. That was delicious," I said. "What was it?"

The twins laughed. "You'll never find out. It's Mum's secret recipe. Even we don't know."

I thought maybe they were joking until Aunt Lucy said, "If I told you, I'd have to kill you."

"Well, whatever it was, it was delicious. Thank you for inviting me."

"The first of many meals together, I hope." Aunt Lucy treated me to one of her huge smiles.

Despite their objections, I insisted that I help the twins with the washing up. Grandma poked her head around the kitchen door to say goodnight. I wasn't sorry to see her go. I'd rather go head-to-head with a serial killer than with Grandma.

The twins must have seen my expression because Amber said, "Don't worry. She scares us too."
"She has a heart of gold though," Pearl said.
"Really?"
"No."
"Does she live close by?"
"Couldn't be any closer. Right next door."
"What about you two? Do you still live with Aunt Lucy?"
The twins looked horrified. "With Mum? No chance. We moved out as soon as we were old enough. We live above the shop."
"Aunt Lucy mentioned that you have a cake shop."
"Cuppy C."
"Sorry?"
"That's the name of our shop." Amber beamed with obvious pride. "'Cuppy C' as in Cuppy Cake. It's a tea room too."
"Nice name."
"You have to come and try our cakes."
"Not tonight. I'm ready to burst."
"Tomorrow then. We open at ten."
"I'll be there."

The atmosphere was much more relaxed after Grandma had left. Aunt Lucy, the twins and I moved into the living room. The twins were keen to pick my brain about life among the humans.
"Have you ever been out of Candlefield?" I asked.
"No, but we want to," Amber said.
"Maybe we could come and visit you?" Pearl looked at me with hopeful eyes.

"Girls! What did I tell you?" Aunt Lucy gave the twins a look.

"But Mum. Now we have a cousin in the human world—"

"Amber!" Aunt Lucy scolded. "Jill has enough on her plate without having to put up with you two."

"You wouldn't mind, Jill, would you?" Amber pressed.

"I suppose it would be okay," I said.

I saw Aunt Lucy roll her eyes. Had I said the wrong thing?

"Thank you!" Amber hurried across the room, followed by Pearl. The two of them hugged me. "Thank you so much."

"When?" Pearl said. "When can we come?"

"I—err—I don't know. I'll—"

"Pearl, stop pressurising her," Aunt Lucy intervened much to my relief.

What had I let myself in for?

At eleven o'clock the twins said their goodnights. I promised to call in their shop the next morning.

"Thank you for today," I said, once Aunt Lucy and I were alone.

"It was my pleasure. Now, let me show you to your room."

The bedroom had obviously once been the twins' room. I got the distinct impression that nothing had been changed since the day they'd moved out. One wall was covered with pictures of pop stars while on the opposite wall were pictures of movie stars. One of the twins was obviously a movie buff—maybe I should introduce her to Mr Ivers. Nah, even I couldn't be that cruel.

I woke up early the next morning. On my way back from the shower, I heard excited voices coming from downstairs. It was Aunt Lucy and the twins. I hadn't expected to see them until I visited their shop later. Once I was dressed, I made my way downstairs to find the three of them at the kitchen table.

"Morning," I said.

"Morning." Came back the chorus.

"Sleep well?" Aunt Lucy walked over to the fridge.

"Like a log."

"Would you like breakfast?"

"Just cereal please."

"Tea?"

"Do you have coffee?"

"Of course."

I took a seat at the table. "I wasn't expecting to see you two until later."

The twins looked at one another and giggled.

"What?"

They giggled some more. It was a little unnerving.

"There you go." Aunt Lucy put a bowl of cereal on the table in front of me.

While I was eating, the twins kept exchanging whispers, and giggling. Something was obviously afoot, but they remained tight-lipped.

When I'd finished, Aunt Lucy took my hand. "Come through to the living room. We have a surprise for you."

"Oh?" I'd never liked surprises. Kathy once threw a surprise birthday party for me, and I'd hated every moment of it.

"Sit there." Aunt Lucy ushered me into the armchair.

"I'll just be a minute."

The twins were giggling again.

"What is it?" I asked, but they giggled all the more. I wasn't going to get any sense out of them.

I heard what sounded like a small stampede. What on earth was going on? The next thing I knew, something big and furry came flying through the door, across the room, and launched itself at me. It knocked me back in the chair, and before I could speak, began to lick my face.

"Get down, Barry," Aunt Lucy shouted. "Get down."

After she'd managed to pull the dog off me, I sat back up in the chair.

"This is Barry." Aunt Lucy still had a firm grip on his collar.

"I'm Barry," Barry said. I still couldn't get used to the idea of talking animals.

"Nice to meet you, Barry." I began to stroke the dog.

"I'm Barry," he repeated, his tail wagging frantically.

"I'm going to let you go," Aunt Lucy said. "But no jumping on Jill. Okay?"

"Okay."

I wasn't convinced, so braced myself for another assault, but Barry was true to his word, and instead rested his head on my knee.

"Do you like him?" Amber asked.

"He's lovely. What is he?"

"I'm right here," Barry said.

"Sorry. I keep forgetting that you can talk. So, what are you?"

"I'm a dog."

"Right. Yeah, of course. Stupid question."

"He's a Labradoodle," Pearl said.

"He's beautiful. Who does he belong to?"

"He's yours." Aunt Lucy patted the dog's back.

"Mine? I can't—"

"I'm yours." Barry licked my hand.

I looked at Amber, then Pearl, and finally at Aunt Lucy. They were all smiles. What was I supposed to do? An image flashed across my mind of Winky launching an attack on poor, sweet Barry. "I'm not allowed to have animals in my flat."

"That's okay, dear," Aunt Lucy said. "Barry will live in Candlefield. Amber, Pearl and I will look after him while you're away. Why don't the three of you take him for a walk?"

"Take me for a walk." Barry jumped up so his front paws were on my knees. "Please!"

Amber linked her arm through my left arm while Pearl took my right arm. I held on to the lead for dear life as we walked to the park, which was only a short distance from Aunt Lucy's house. Once we were there, Barry began to pull on the lead.

"Let me go! I want to run!"

I wasn't sure. What if he ran away?

"He'll be okay," Amber said.

I took a deep breath, and unclipped the lead. Barry shot off across the huge grassed area.

"Do you like him?" Pearl asked.

"He's lovely. I've never had a dog before. I'm not sure how often I'll get to see him though."

"We'll take good care of him while you're away. How often do you think you'll be able to visit Candlefield?"

Washbridge was my home, and probably always would

be, but I was already beginning to feel a connection to my new family. And now I had a dog to consider.

"I'm not sure. I wouldn't want to impose on Aunt Lucy too often."

"You could always stay with Grandma," Amber said.

They both laughed when they saw the horrified look on my face.

"Kidding. We wouldn't do that to you. There's a spare room at our place that you can use when you come over. We'll show it to you later. As payment, maybe you can help out in Cuppy C sometimes."

"Yeah, maybe." Me? Work in the tea room? That had disaster written all over it.

"Barry! Come here!" We'd been in the park for just over half an hour, and Barry had barely stopped running for more than a couple of minutes during that time. I was exhausted just watching him. "Barry!" I shouted again in vain.

It was fifteen minutes later when I finally managed to grab a hold of him.

Chapter 19

Aunt Lucy said she'd look after Barry while the twins gave me a tour of their shop. Cuppy C was on the east side of Candlefield. The huge windows made the ideal showcase for the beautiful cakes inside. The sign above the door displayed a picture of a strawberry cupcake.

"Do you bake the cakes yourself?"

"Heavens no." Pearl laughed.

For some reason I'd assumed the twins were bakers.

"We can't bake to save our lives," Pearl said. "We use a number of different bakers. Mostly small concerns. Our main delivery should be here in about ten minutes."

"Do either of you have a boyfriend?" I asked, while trying to balance two boxes of cakes.

They both giggled. They giggled a lot.

"I'm seeing the most handsome man in Candlefield," Pearl said.

"No you're not," Amber objected. "You can't possibly think Alan is more handsome than William."

"I don't think. I know."

"You're crazy. And jealous!"

This outburst took me by surprise. Until then, I'd only ever seen a close bond between the twins. Now, suddenly, lines had been drawn.

"Jealous of William?" Pearl snapped. "Now I know you're insane."

"Girls, girls." I stepped between them before they began to scratch each other's eyes out. "Are Alan and William—?" I hesitated. "I mean to say, what are—what kind of—?"

"Alan is a vampire," Pearl said.

"And William is a werewolf." Amber screwed up her nose at her twin sister. There was obviously more rivalry between the two of them than I'd realised.

"Do different types of sups often date one another?"

"Yeah. It's quite common. What about you, Jill?" Pearl asked.

"What about me?"

"Are you in a relationship?"

"No. I'm taking a break." See how I made it sound like it was by choice. "I have a bad habit of picking losers."

"Is there anyone you have your eye on?" Amber asked.

I hesitated a few seconds too long. "No."

"You can tell us."

"There really isn't. It's just—nothing."

"Come on, Jill. Spill the beans."

"Okay. A while back, a new detective moved to the Washbridge area. I thought he was kind of—"

"Hot?" Pearl giggled.

"Yeah. But that was before I discovered that he was a complete asshat."

"Did you go out with him?"

"No. We never dated, but my work brings me into contact with him—unfortunately. He isn't my number one fan, and he takes every opportunity to tell me so."

"But you still have the hots for him?"

"No, it's just—" This had been bugging me ever since that day at the police station.

"What? We won't tell. Promise."

"I used the 'mind read' spell on him. I thought that if I could make him think about the case I was working on, he might reveal information that would help me. But when I saw what was on his mind — "

"He was thinking about you, wasn't he?"

I nodded.

"What was it? Something depraved and disgusting?"

"No! No! Nothing like that. He was thinking what it would be like to kiss me."

"That's good isn't it?"

"No. It's not good. It's terrible. I hate the man." What? It's true. I do hate him and I hadn't once wondered what it might be like to kiss him. Not once. Ever.

By a quarter to ten, all of the cakes were on display.

"Thanks for your help," Amber said. "As payment, you can have your choice of cake."

It wasn't an easy decision, but in the end I decided upon the double-chocolate.

"Would you like to see your room?" Amber asked.

I wasn't ready to think of it as 'my room' yet, but I didn't think it would do any harm to take a look. "Don't you need to open up the shop?"

"Pearl can look after things down here, can't you Pearl?"

"Yes, Amber dear." She sneered, "I usually do anyway."

"You do not!"

I was starting to rethink my initial impression that the twins lived together in blissful harmony.

The space above the shop covered two floors. On one floor was the kitchen and living room. On the top floor were three bedrooms, and a bathroom.

"This is my room." Amber pushed open the door. I now knew which of them was the movie buff. "And this pig-sty is Pearl's." She pushed open the next door and held her nose. I peered inside expecting to see a scene of devastation, but apart from a few clothes in one corner, it was perfectly tidy. If Amber thought Pearl was untidy, she should meet Kathy.

"And this will be your room." Amber stepped aside, so I could see. "We can change the colour if you don't like it."

"It's lovely." The lemon coloured room appeared to have been recently decorated, and had a new carpet smell.

"You *will* come to stay won't you?" Amber said.

"Of course. As often as I can, but I do have a business to run and a family back in Washbridge."

"Mum said you have a sister."

"Kathy. She has two fantastic kids."

"Will we get to meet them when we come over?"

"Sure."

"Thank goodness you're here," Mrs V greeted me the next morning. "That cat has been driving me insane."

Nothing new there then. "Anything else I should know about?"

"Not really." She shrugged.

"No phone calls? No new enquiries?"

"No."

I sighed. If business didn't pick up soon I'd be in big trouble. Maybe I should give it all up and move to Candlefield.

"Thank goodness you're here," Winky said. "That woman has been driving me insane." He rubbed up against my leg and I saw his nose twitch. "What's that?"

"What?"

"That smell."

"What smell?"

"Dog." Winky took a step back, and gave me the evil eye. "You smell of dog."

"That's Barry."

"Barry?"

"He's a Labradoodle."

"You have a dog? I thought you said you couldn't have pets at your flat. You've been lying to me."

Winky could be scary when he was mad, and right now he was livid.

"He's not my dog. Not really. He — err — he belongs to a friend. I was just visiting."

Winky looked unconvinced. I needed to change the subject. "Are you hungry?"

"Starving."

"Come on then. Let's give you some food."

All was forgiven.

Or so I thought.

Mrs V had placed a copy of the Bugle on my desk. The headline read 'Face of the Animal'. The article covered the arrest of Martin Kilburn who had now been charged with all three murders. According to the article, the arrest had followed a tip off from a tattoo artist. How accurate this information was, I'd no way of knowing — this was the Bugle after all. Apparently Kilburn had asked for a tattoo of a fox. The owner of the tattoo parlour had noticed that he already had a tattoo of a lamb and a lion, so had contacted the police.

The article included two photographs of Kilburn. He was bare-chested, and appeared to be showing off his tattoos to the camera. In the first photo he was facing the camera; in the second he had his back to it. His torso was covered in numerous tattoos, but there was no sign of a lamb, lion or fox. But then, the caption did state that the photos had been taken the previous year. The tattoos on his arms were only partially visible, but by studying the two photographs, I was able to make out one in particular. It was on his left arm, and was of two crossed daggers. That matched the description given by the eye-witness at Pauline Lyon's house. It looked as though Maxwell might have got his man after all.

So what was bugging me? Something didn't feel right. I studied the photos again—checking every individual tattoo. There was no single large tattoo. Instead, there were clusters of small ones.

Wait a minute—these weren't just random tattoos.

"I'm going to the police station," I said as I hurried past Mrs V.

"To see Detective Maxwell? Such a nice young man. You should wear that red dress. The one you bought last Christmas."

"Yeah—I don't think so."

"Do you want to take a scarf for him?" She pulled open the bottom drawer of her desk.

"I think he's good for scarves, thanks."

"Jack Maxwell, please," I said to the young police officer who was manning the front desk.

"Do you have an appointment?"

"No, but it'll only take a minute."

"What's it in connection with?"

"I have some information relating to the 'Animal' case."

"And you are?"

"Jill Gooder."

Her expression changed the moment she heard my name. I assumed that meant I was on some kind of blacklist.

"What kind of information?"

"I'd rather speak to Detective Maxwell."

She glared at me for a few moments, and then made a call. "Hi, I have a Jill Gooder at the front desk." She listened for a few seconds. "What shall I tell her then?" Once the call had ended, she gave me a withering look, and said, "Sorry. He can't see you."

"It's important."

She shrugged. "I can get someone else to take the information from you if you wish?"

"Forget it."

There had to be a way to get to Maxwell. I parked in the supermarket car park, which was opposite the police station. At ten minutes before midday, I saw Maxwell's car appear. From that distance, I couldn't be sure if he was alone in the car or not. It took me a few seconds to force my way across the traffic, and I almost lost sight of his vehicle. I tucked in three cars behind him and followed.

After ten minutes, he pulled into the car park of the Whistling Pig pub. I drove around to the rear of the building, and parked as close as I could to the door. Before he'd even got out of his car, I'd cast the 'faster' spell and made my way inside. By the time Maxwell walked through the door, I was already seated at the bar.

"What are you doing here?" he snapped.

"Getting a drink. What about you?"

I could see the cogs in his mind working overtime.

Could my being there really have been a coincidence? For a moment, I thought he might turn around and walk back out.

"Jack!" The barman greeted him. "Your usual?"

Jack looked at the barman, and then at me. I still wasn't sure if he'd stay or not.

"Yes please, Gary."

"*I* was here first, *actually*," I chimed in.

The barman looked at Maxwell.

"You'd better serve the *lady* first." If looks could kill, I'd have been a goner.

"Thank you. I'll have whatever the detective is having." Maxwell sat down on the stool next to mine. "How did you know I'd be here?"

"I didn't." I lied. "Coincidence I guess." And a little bit of magic.

"I don't believe in coincidence. Didn't you come into the station earlier this morning?"

"Yes, I did. They said you were busy."

"I am."

"So I see."

"It's my lunch break."

"There you go." The barman placed two soda and limes on the bar in front of us.

"I see you're on the hard stuff." I raised a glass. "Cheers!"

Maxwell scowled. "What do you want?"

"What makes you think I want anything? I just popped in here for a bite—"

"Don't give me that, Gooder. What do you want?"

There was something distinctly sexy about him when he was mad—not that I'd noticed or anything. I was way too busy hating his guts.

"You've got the wrong man."

"What are you talking about?"

"For the 'Animal' murders. Kilburn didn't do it."

"Really? And you know this how?"

"The tattoos."

"The tattoos are precisely why we know he did do it."

"You mean the lamb, lion and fox?"

"Plus the tattoo on his arm."

"The daggers? That's it? That's all you have?"

"Then there's the small matter of his confession." His smirk was back big time.

"His confession isn't worth the paper it's written on."

The barman placed a ploughman's lunch in front of each of us. Maxwell took a bite of his.

"Says who?" he munched.

"Says me. The man is obviously some kind of nut job."

"He killed three people. Of course he's a nut job."

"Martin Kilburn didn't kill anyone. He gets his jollies from stalking serial killers. Check his tattoos. Almost every one is related to a serial killer. Remember the 'Razor'? That's on his left shoulder. The 'Reaper' is on his chest. The 'Dorm Killer' is on his back. Do you want me to go on? If you don't believe me, go check them out. The 'Animal' tattoos were just the latest addition to his gallery."

Maxwell was silent for a long moment, and then said, "That changes nothing. We still have the cross daggers tattoo, and his confession. Kilburn did it."

Chapter 20

I could have let it go at that. After all, everyone was happy. Jack Maxwell was happy because he thought he'd got his man. Danny Peterson was happy because he believed his girlfriend's killer had been caught, and his serial killer theory had been proven correct. Even Martin Kilburn was happy because he was in the limelight. So why wasn't I happy?

It just didn't sit right with me. It was all way too neat and convenient.

"Hi!" Kathy greeted me. She looked harassed as usual. "Come in."

"Sorry, I should have called first."

"Don't be daft. I need some grown-up company." She was picking up Lego pieces as we walked through to the living room. "How was Candlefield?"

"Good. Really good, actually. Shall I make us a coffee?"

"That would be great, thanks," she said while still collecting Lego pieces. "I'm sure this stuff is breeding."

"So? What's your new family like?" Kathy sipped her coffee. "Biscuit?"

I declined the offer. Custard creams, digestives, ginger nuts and jammy dodgers—all in the same biscuit barrel—just wrong. "Aunt Lucy is a darling, and Amber and Pearl—"

"Amber and Pearl? That's their names? Seriously?"

"Yeah. They're identical twins and really sweet."

"What about Grandma?"

A shudder ran down my spine. "She's a bit scary." Make

that a *lot* scary.

"How do you mean?"

"You'd understand if you saw her."

"When do I get to visit Candlefield?"

I'd been dreading that question. How was I meant to explain to Kathy why she couldn't visit Candlefield when I wasn't allowed to tell her about the whole 'witch' thing?

"Amber and Pearl want to come to Washbridge. I told them all about the kids and they can't wait to meet you all."

"Really? That would be great."

"The kids will love them."

I'd dodged the bullet for now, but Kathy wasn't stupid — she'd soon realise that I was hiding something.

"Are the kids okay?" When in doubt, change the subject. Clever eh?

"They're great. Especially when they're asleep." She dunked a ginger biscuit into her coffee.

Yuk! She knew how much I hated it when she did that.

"What?" Kathy said through a mouthful of mushy ginger biscuit.

"Nothing."

"I saw you pull a face. It tastes better when it's been dunked."

"It's disgusting." I had to look away.

"It's yummy. You should try it."

"I think I'll pass."

"Please yourself." She shoved the rest of the biscuit into her mouth. "I seyo caut—"

"What? I can't understand a word you are saying. Wait until you've finished eating."

"There! All gone. Happy now?"

"Why do you have to do that? It's gross."

"You have biscuit issues." Kathy glanced at the biscuit barrel, but thankfully thought better of helping herself to another one. "I see they caught your serial killer."

"Maybe."

"You don't sound convinced."

"I'm not. I told Maxwell that I thought he had the wrong man."

"I bet that went down well. What makes you think that?"

I told her about the guy's collection of serial killer tattoos, and my concern over the lack of any other evidence.

"What are you going to do about it?"

That was a good question. Danny Peterson considered the case closed, so what would be the point in my pursuing it any further? It's not like I'd get paid. I'd have to be stupid and incredibly stubborn not to let it go.

Stupid *and* stubborn? Did someone call?

"What did you do to that cat?" Mrs V said when I arrived at the office.

"Nothing. Why?"

"He's gone insane."

"How can you tell?"

"You'll see."

I didn't like the sound of that. I braced myself; this wasn't going to be good. I walked through to my office, and closed the door behind me.

Winky was curled in a ball on the window sill—fast asleep. I glanced around, but there was no obvious sign of carnage. I didn't get it. What could he have done that had upset Mrs V so much? Aside from breathing? Oh well, whatever it was, everything seemed to be okay. And then I saw it.

"What the—? Winky!"

"What's up?" He half-opened his good eye.

"I'm going to kill you!"

"Take a chill pill."

"Take a—?" I ran my fingers across my desk. The once-smooth surface now felt like a cheese grater. "What did you do to my desk?"

"You mean my scratching board?"

"Scratching—? Come here!" I reached out to grab him, but he was too quick. He'd jumped off the window sill, ducked under the desk, and was now mono-staring at me from the other side of the room. "Why did you do this?"

"One word."

"What?"

"Barry."

"You destroyed my desk because you were jealous?"

"I would never have agreed to live with you if I'd known you were going to have a dog."

"*You* wouldn't have agreed to live with *me*?"

"Exactly!"

"There's no exactly about it. Firstly, I chose you. And secondly—" I couldn't believe I was trying to justify myself to a cat. "I've already told you. Barry isn't my dog!"

"Whose dog is he then?"

I wasn't supposed to tell humans that I was a witch or about Candlefield. What about cats? Could I tell them?

Why didn't this whole 'witch' thing come with some kind of instruction manual? I daren't risk it.

"He belongs to my cousins, Amber and Pearl. I went to visit them."

"Bad names."

"Yes, well, anyway—Barry is their dog, but they said I should think of him as mine." This sounded lame even to me. "My lease doesn't allow me to have pets—any pets. If it did, I'd take you home. Obviously."

"Hmm."

"It's true. I'm sorry if I upset you." Why was I apologising to him after he'd destroyed my desk?

"You got any food?"

"There's a tin in the cupboard."

"Go get it and then we'll say no more about this."

"Okay. Thanks!"

Bettered by a cat. My fall from grace was now complete.

I felt a little self-conscious, but at least there was only Winky around to witness my crazy. "Mum?" I glanced around. "Are you here?"

Winky glanced at me, but I ignored him.

"Mum!"

"What is it, Jill?" My mother's ghost appeared next to the window.

Winky hissed in her general direction, but then went back to his food.

"Can he see you?" I asked.

"No, but he can probably sense my presence. Animals are much more sensitive than humans." She screwed up her face. "Ugly isn't he?"

"That's not very nice." True, but not nice. "He does his

best with what he has."

"You called me."

"Yes, sorry. It's just that I don't know what to do about Kathy."

"Is she all right?"

"Yeah, she's fine. It's just that I told her about Candlefield before I realised that I *shouldn't* tell her about Candlefield."

"You told her you're a witch?"

"No, no, nothing like that. I just mentioned that my new family lived there. I wish I hadn't because she's already asking if she can go to Candlefield with me. I don't know what to do. What can I say to her?"

"That's an easy one to solve. You need the 'forget' spell — it's in your book. "Now what page is it on? I forget." She laughed. "Sorry, my little joke."

I forced a smile. She and Kathy would make a great double-act.

"Oh, yes. Page sixty-seven."

"How does it work?"

"The book will explain it better than I can, but essentially if you ever find yourself in a tight spot, and she's asking you about Candlefield, you cast the spell and voila!"

"Voila?"

"Precisely. She'll forget what she was talking about, and you'll be able to change the subject."

"Would it work when she talks about beanies too?"

"Sorry?"

"Never mind. That sounds ideal."

Chapter 21

"Mrs V, I have a little job for you." I didn't like having to interrupt her knitting, but sometimes needs must.
"Do you want me to order you a new desk, dear?"
Why does everyone have to be a comedian?
"Will you contact Mr Lyon and Mr Lamb, and see if you can arrange a time later today when I can go and see them, please?"
"Certainly dear. Shall I ask them if they'd like a scarf?"
"Why not?"

My phone rang.
"Jill!" The high pitched voice almost shattered my ear drum. "It's Amber!"
"Oh? Hi, Amber." I held the phone two inches from my ear.
"And Pearl!"
"I'll do the talking," Amber said.
"She's my cousin too."
"It's my news!"
"Girls!" I interrupted. "What can I do for you?" And to think my first impression had been how well they got on together.
"You said we could come to Washbridge soon," Amber said.
"Yes, I suppose I did."
"Well—" Amber giggled.
"What?"
"We were wondering—" She giggled some more. Now, she was making me nervous. "Could we come over tomorrow night?"

"Tomorrow?" I said. "Like the day after today?"

"Yeah. If that's okay? We wouldn't normally ask, but I have some exciting news."

"Really, what's that?"

"She's got engaged!" Pearl shouted from the background.

"I wanted to tell her," Amber complained.

"You were too slow."

"Engaged?" I managed to get a word in. "To William?"

"Yeah. Can we come over? I want to show you the ring."

"It looks cheap!" Pearl shouted.

"It does *not* look cheap. It's beautiful."

"Looks like it fell out of a lucky bag."

"I'm going to kill you, Pearl."

"What did Aunt Lucy say?" I asked.

"About us coming over? She's fine with it."

"I meant about your engagement. What did she say when you told her?"

"I kinda haven't *actually* told her yet. I'm going to though—soon. So, is it okay for us to come over?"

"I've actually arranged to visit my sister tomorrow night," I lied.

"That's great, we'll come with you."

"With me?"

"Yeah."

"To Kathy's?"

"Yeah. It'll be great. We can't wait to meet the kids."

The kids and the twins in the same room? *Great* wasn't the first word that came to mind.

"Is that okay?" Amber said.

"Please say yes," Pearl shouted.

"Yeah. Sure. Why not? I'd better give you my sister's

address."

"No need. We'll find it. We'll stay overnight at your place and go back the following day, if that's okay?"

"At my place?" Oh dear. "Sure."

"See you later."

What had I let myself in for? When I'd told the twins that I'd arranged to go to Kathy's, I was kind of hoping that might put them off. It wasn't that I didn't want to see them—I did—but I'd hoped to have longer to build myself up to it.

I called Kathy.

"Do you have plans for tomorrow night?"

"You only ask if I have plans when you want a favour," she said.

"That's not true."

"What about the time you wanted me to wait in at your place for the new sofa to be delivered?"

"I was on a stake-out."

"Or the time that you wanted me to take that ugly cat of yours to the vet?"

"First of all, Winky is not ugly. And I'd have taken him, but I had to visit a client."

"So you don't want a favour?"

"No, and I'm very hurt that you'd think so. I was just checking if you fancied company tomorrow night?"

"Sure. We never go out on a Friday night. Or Monday, or Tuesday, Wednesday, Thursday—"

"So it's okay if we come over then?"

"Why not? Hold on—*we*? Have you got yourself a man at last? Jack Maxwell?"

"What do you mean at last? And no, it's not a man. I

thought it would be nice for you to meet my cousins."

"The twins? Opal and Diamond?"

"Pearl and Amber. Is that okay?"

"Yeah. I'd love to meet them. Maybe they'll invite me to visit Candlefield because it doesn't look like my own sister is ever likely to."

I ignored the not-so-subtle dig at me.

"How long will they be over for?" Kathy asked.

"Just overnight. They'll be going back on Saturday."

"They're staying at your place?" I heard her laugh.

"What's wrong with that?"

"Aren't you worried they'll mess up your precious show home?"

"I don't know what you mean." I knew only too well what she meant. As much as I loved Kathy's kids, I rarely (never) invited them over to my place. What? That doesn't make me a bad person. I'd seen the devastation they could wreak. Amber and Pearl were adults — they'd have more respect for my property. Wouldn't they? Now she had me worried. Maybe I should pack away some of my ornaments.

"I'm sorry about the desk." Winky jumped onto the chair opposite me.

Was I hearing things or had he just apologised?

"So you should be. I'm going to have to get someone in to remove these scratches."

"Why don't you throw the old thing away and get a new one?"

"This is an antique, and besides it belonged to my father."

"So? It's decrepit. Like that old bag out there. You should

get rid of her too while you're at it."

That was more like the Winky I loved to hate.

"Mrs V isn't going anywhere. You two will have to learn to get along together."

"She hates me. When you're not here, she tortures me with her knitting needles."

"You're such a liar." I hoped it was a lie, but I wouldn't have put it past her.

Mrs V hadn't managed to contact Mr Lyon, but Harry Lamb had said I could go over straight away.

"Thank you," Mr Lamb said when I passed him the scarf. "I didn't really need this, but your receptionist was quite insistent."

"Sorry about that. She can be a little pushy. Have you heard from the police since the arrest?"

"Nothing. All I know is what I've seen on the news. Do you know anything about this Kilburn chap?"

"Only that he has some kind of serial killer fetish. And, apparently, he's confessed."

"Do *you* think he did it?"

"I don't know. I'd like to see more by way of proof."

"What do the others say? Geoff and what's his name?"

"Danny Peterson. Danny seems happy about the arrest. I haven't spoken to Geoffrey Lyon yet."

"You must have your doubts or you wouldn't be here."

"I wanted to ask you about something your wife's brother said."

"Derek? You've met him then?"

I nodded.

"Watching him destroy himself broke Trisha's heart.

They'd always been so close."

"He told me that Trisha was thinking of leaving you."

Harry Lamb shook his head. I'd expected him to react angrily, but instead he looked sad. "Derek is a mess. Half of the time he doesn't know what he's saying."

"He looked in a bad way."

"That's why Trisha spent so much time around there. She tried to help, but it was hopeless. Most of the time, he just threw her kindness back in her face. Would you like a cup of tea or coffee?"

"No thanks." I noticed the photo album open on the table.

"Memories," he said. "That's all I have now. Sit down, let me show you."

How could I say no? The man was hurting so badly, it seemed a small sacrifice to spend a few minutes with him.

"That was when we went to London for the weekend three years ago. And that was our anniversary party."

"Your wife changed her hairstyle a lot."

"She used to. Not so much in recent years though. Back then, Derek used to try out his new styles on her. Trisha didn't mind because he was so talented. He even won a few awards. You probably saw his trophies when you went to see him."

"Her brother is a hairdresser?"

"He was. Now he just spends all day drinking."

I checked in with Mrs V. She still hadn't been able to get in touch with Mr Lyon. My next phone call was to Janet Wesley, Mrs Lyon's sister. She was able to provide me with the name of the salon where Pauline Lyon had had her bad hair day.

Twists Hair Salon was only a short walk from my office.
"Good afternoon, madam." The receptionist glanced
disapprovingly at my hair. "Do you have an
appointment?"
"I'd like to speak to the manager, please."
"Who should I say wants to see her?"
"I do." What? She deserved that for the way she'd
looked at my hair.
The manager was all smiles and curls. "How can I help?"
"I'm a private investigator." That usually impressed
people. "Can I have a few words in private?"
I followed her to a small office at the back of the shop.
"I wanted to ask you about an incident that took place
here some weeks ago now."
"What kind of incident?" She kept glancing at my hair.
Surely it wasn't that bad.
"One of your customers made a complaint against a
member of your staff."
"We get the occasional complaint. Nothing serious
though. Usually one of the younger girls running their
mouths off. The stuff some of these youngsters talk
about; it embarrasses our older ladies."
"It was a little more serious than that. One of your
stylists was drunk, and ruined—"
"How did you hear about that?"
"That's not important."
"It was terrible. The poor lady was distraught, and I
don't blame her."
"Mrs Lyon?"
"I don't remember her name, but she's never been back

since. Can't say I blame her. It was partly my fault. I should have sacked him the first time it happened, but he begged for another chance and big softy that I am I—"

"What's his name? The stylist?"
"Antoine."
Damn it, I'd been so sure.
"Right, I'm sorry to have troubled you." I started for the door.
"Of course, that isn't his real name. We all use 'stage names'. His real name is Derek Cairn."

"What do you want?" Cairn said. He looked more awake this time, but smelled much worse.
"Can I come in?"
"What for?"
"I want to see your trophies." I'd already cast the 'power' spell, so when I pushed the door it sent him flying backwards across the floor.
"What do you think you're doing?" he said, as I walked past him.
"I've already told you. I want to see your trophies."
He picked himself up, and followed me into the living room.
"These were your glory days, eh Derek?" I picked up one of the trophies. "Or should I call you Antoine?"
"Put that down or I'll call the police."
"I seriously doubt it. When did it all start to go wrong? When did the drink take over?"
"Get out!" he shouted. "I mean it." He grabbed a pair of scissors from the table.
"Are they what you used on Pauline Lyon?"

"Get out!" He pointed the scissors at me.

"And on Trisha?"

The colour drained from his face. The scissors fell to the floor.

"Why did you do it Derek? Trisha was the one person in the world who still loved you. Why kill your sister?"

The tears gathered in his eyes, and he slumped down onto the floor. "I didn't mean to."

"So how did it happen?"

"I begged her." He sniffled. "I begged her, but she wouldn't listen."

"She was going to tell the police, wasn't she?"

He didn't answer. I leaned over and pulled up the sleeve of his tee-shirt.

Just as I'd suspected.

Chapter 22

"What's Amber's fiancé like?" Kathy shouted from the bedroom. I'd arrived at her place just after six. I wanted to be sure I was there ahead of the twins.

"I haven't met him, yet."

"Don't you know *anything* about him?"

I believe he enjoys a full moon. "Not really."

"Do you think I'll get an invite to the wedding? I am family after all." Kathy walked into the living room. She'd spent the last hour getting ready—I'd spent two minutes brushing my hair.

"Give them a chance—they've only just got engaged."

"I do love a good wedding."

"I know." I hated them. Expensive waste of time if you ask me—not that anyone did.

"I hope the twins arrive before Pete gets back with the kids." Kathy took a bottle of wine out of the fridge. "It'd be nice to have a few minutes to get to know them before all hell breaks loose. What time did they say they'd be here?"

"They didn't."

"I hope you didn't give them directions." She laughed. "If you did, they'll never find their way."

"You're *so* funny!"

"You couldn't even find Candlefield. Remember?"

"Are you starting with the wine already?"

"Are you changing the subject?"

I was. "No. I just don't want you drunk before the twins get here."

"I need a drink. And you will too once the kids get back." She held up the bottle.

"Just a small one then."

"Where are they?" Lizzie demanded, as she rushed into the room. "Have they brought us a present?"
Peter had returned with the kids. If the plan had been to tire them out, he'd failed miserably. Mikey was running around the living room with a plane held high in his hand. Lizzie was bouncing up and down next to me on the sofa — I was beginning to feel sea sick.
"They're not here yet," Kathy said, grabbing hold of Lizzie and pulling her off the sofa. "And don't go expecting presents."
"Dad said they'd bring us a present," Mikey said.
Kathy glared at Peter.
"What?" He shrugged.
"If they don't bring presents," Kathy took a slug of wine, "it's on you."
She needn't have worried because when the twins arrived just before seven-thirty, Amber had a huge package for Lizzie, and Pearl had a slightly smaller one for Mikey.
"Lego Spaceport!" Lizzie screamed.
"I've got a remote control car!" Mikey sent the red four-by-four crashing into Kathy's shin.
"Take those into your bedrooms, please. I'll bring your supper through to you. Wait! Have you said thank you to Amber and Pearl?"
"Thank you!"
"Thanks!"

The twins were dressed in polka dots — again. Amber wore a blue dress with white dots; Pearl's was white with blue dots. Amber wore her hair down; Pearl had hers in a bun. At least it would be easy enough to tell them apart.

"Can I see the ring?" Kathy said. It hadn't occurred to me to ask, but then I'd never been one to get excited about other people's jewellery.

Amber stretched out her hand.

"It's gorgeous," Kathy cooed. "Isn't it, Jill?"

"Yeah. It's lovely." Seen one, seen them all.

"It's too tight for her finger," Pearl said.

"It is *not!*" Amber turned on her sister.

I wasn't about to take sides, but Pearl did have a point. The ring did look incredibly tight.

"What's your fiancé's name?" Kathy asked.

"William." Amber beamed.

"What does he do?"

Please don't say he's a werewolf. Please don't say he's a werewolf.

"He's a were—"

Oh no.

"Warehouse manager. Well, assistant manager actually."

"He wears a yellow overall." Pearl sniggered.

"It suits him."

"He looks like a banana."

"What about you, Pearl?" Kathy stepped in. She was accustomed to playing the role of mediator with her own kids. "Do you have a boyfriend?"

"Alan. He's in finance," she said proudly.

"Finance?" Amber scoffed. "He works in a pawn shop."

Pearl ignored her sister. "Would you like to see a photo of him?" She took out her phone.

"Of course we would, wouldn't we, Jill?"

"Sure." I'd always thought it was impossible to take a photo of a vampire. Perhaps I was getting photos confused with mirrors.

"He's very handsome," Kathy said.

"Very." For a bloodsucking creature of the night.

Not to be outdone, Amber pulled up a photo of William.

"You're both very lucky girls," Kathy said.

To save Kathy from having to cook, we'd ordered in pizza. Thankfully, the kids were still enthralled by their new toys, so were happy to eat in their rooms.

"Will you have time to show us around tomorrow, Jill?" Amber asked through a mouthful of pizza. "We'd love to see the shops."

"I'd rather see the sights," Pearl said.

"Shops!"

"Sights!"

"I'm sure there'll be time for both," I intervened. So much for *my* Saturday.

"I might join you," Kathy said. "You'll have the kids, Pete, won't you?"

"Do I have a choice?" He grinned. If I knew Peter, he'd take the kids over a shopping trip any day of the week.

At eight-thirty, the kids were told to say their goodnights. Much moaning and groaning ensued, but eventually they gave us all a goodnight kiss.

"Night!" The twins shouted.

"Thanks for the present," Lizzie called back.

"Thanks for the car," Mikey shouted.

Peter disappeared into the bedroom to read them a bedtime story.

"Now then girls," Kathy said to the twins. "I've asked Jill

when I can visit you in Candlefield, but she keeps fobbing me off."

The twins both looked at me, unsure what to say. I gave them my '*I got this*' look, and cast the 'forget' spell.

Kathy shook her head. "What was I talking about?"

The spell had done its job.

"You were asking the twins which shops they wanted to visit tomorrow," I prompted.

"Was I? Yes, of course."

Once the kids were asleep, Peter joined us. The five of us talked until after midnight. Well, when I say the five of us talked, Peter and I were pretty much consigned to the sidelines while Kathy and the twins planned the next day's shopping trip like a military exercise.

The twins and I arrived back at my flat just before one in the morning. I was dead on my feet — the twins were still as lively (noisy) as ever. They shared a double bed in the spare bedroom, which was right next to mine. It was almost two o'clock before they finally fell asleep. That's when the snoring began. In stereo.

"Morning, Jill." The first of the twins surfaced at seven the next morning. She had a bad case of bed-hair, so I had to check for the beauty spot before concluding it was Amber.

"Morning, Amber."

"Sleep well?" She yawned.

"Yeah." For about twenty minutes. "You?"

"Pearl kept me awake with her snoring."

"I wasn't snoring." Pearl appeared behind Amber. "It was you."

"I do not snore."

"Breakfast?" I asked. It was going to be a long day.

"Just coffee for me, please," Amber said.

"Tea and toast for me, please." Pearl pushed past her sister. "I'll make it."

"It's okay." I jumped off the stool. "You're my guests. I've got it."

"Could I have toast too?" Amber said. "With lots of jam."

"I thought you were on a diet?" Pearl joined her sister at the kitchen table.

"I never said that!"

"Right, I must be hearing things then."

"How do you like your toast?" I shouted.

"Crispy, please," Amber said.

"Lightly toasted for me, please."

"I love your flat," Amber said, dropping crumbs onto the floor, as we moved through to the living room.

"Thank you."

"Me too." Pearl walked across the room to the stereo. "What's this?" I cringed as she ran her buttery fingers over the polished top.

"It's a stereo. It plays vinyl."

"Vinyl what?"

"Records, music."

"Like CD's?"

"Yeah. A bit like CD's but older."

"Cool!"

My poor flat. My poor, poor flat. By the time we left, the place was a tip. There went *my* Sunday—I'd have to spend the whole day tidying and cleaning. For the life of me, I couldn't understand why the twins had decided to live together. They argued all the time—about anything and everything. My head was spinning.

I didn't have the shopping gene. Kathy, on the other hand, enjoyed nothing better. She'd think nothing of spending six hours looking for the right outfit. I trailed along behind the three of them as they cooed over dresses, and handbags, and make-up and a million other things. Would they notice if I sneaked away? It was very tempting, but Kathy would never have forgiven me.

"Do you think Alan would like these?" Pearl held up a skimpy, lacy lingerie set.

"Any man would love those." Kathy grinned.

What about vampires, I wondered.

"You aren't a D cup!" Amber laughed.

"I am too!" Pearl's cheeks reddened.

"You're the exact same size as me, and I'm not a D."

"I've grown recently."

"Let's compare."

"Whoa!" I stepped in between them. "Let's not. I'm ready for a sit down. How about a coffee?"

"Come on girls," Kathy said. "Your cousin Jill is getting too old for this shopping lark. She needs regular breaks."

I glared at Kathy. She ignored me. At least world war D had been averted.

"These aren't as nice as ours," Pearl said as she sampled the cakes.

"Agreed." Amber had jam on her top lip.

At least the twins could agree on something.

"Who's looking after the shop?" I said.

"Shop?" Kathy's ears pricked up at the word 'shop'.

"The girls have a cake shop and tea room."

"Cuppy C." Pearl beamed.

"Cuppa tea?" Kathy said.

"Not cuppa tea," I corrected her. "Cuppy C. C for cake."

"You're no bigger than a C," Amber said to her sister.

"I am too."

After that particular storm in a 'C' cup was over, we moved on to the high street. Within an hour, the twins and Kathy were laden with carrier bags. Peter *would* be pleased.

"Why don't *you* buy something, Jill?" Pearl asked, swapping the bags from one hand to the other.

"Jill doesn't do 'high street'," Kathy said. "She buys all her clothes from a little boutique called 'Stuck in the Sixties'."

I ignored the jibe. I couldn't help it if I was the only one in the family with taste.

The three of them were waiting in line to pay for their purchases. I was bringing up the rear trying not to look as bored as I felt.

"I wish we had those in Candlefield," Amber said, pointing to Kathy's credit card.

"You're better off without them," I said. I dreaded to think what Kathy's next credit card bill would look like.

"How can you say that?" Pearl was staring at the card. "It's way better than money."

"We wouldn't have to work." Amber was drooling over the card too.

"Hold on," I said. "You do realise that you still have to pay for everything you buy, don't you?"

"Don't be silly, Jill," Pearl said. "You just have to give

them your card. Look!"
Perhaps it was just as well that plastic hadn't made it to
Candlefield.

"Ouch!" Amber cried out.
"Are you okay?" Kathy said.
"It's her own fault," Pearl said.
Amber had caught her finger on the counter top.
"Let me see." Kathy was used to dealing with her kids'
cuts and scrapes. "That looks sore."
It did. Her ring finger, now minus the ring, was red and
swollen.
"She had to use the soap to get the ring off this
morning," Pearl said. "I told her it was too tight."
"Shut up, Pearl," Amber snapped.
"It'll be okay in a few days," Kathy said. "You'd better
get the ring resized before you put it on again though."
I stared at Amber's finger, and something clicked.
"Sorry, I have to go," I said.
"Jill?" Kathy looked daggers at me. "You can't just—"
"I have to. Something urgent just came up on one of my
cases."
I could tell that Kathy didn't believe a word I was saying.
"Girls, I'm really sorry about this," I said.
"Don't worry about it, Jill," Pearl said. "Go catch the bad
guy!"
"Yeah," Amber chirped. "We'll be fine. Make sure you
come and visit us soon!"
"I will. I promise." I turned to Kathy. "Sorry."
"You and me are going to have words later," she said in
a whisper.

"Is that Josie Trent?" I had to shout to make myself heard.

"Speaking."

Josie Trent was still on board The Grand Oceans, a luxury liner, which was somewhere off the coast of Barbados.

"My name is Jill Gooder. I'm a private investigator. I'm investigating the murder of Caroline Fox."

"Poor Caroline. I still can't believe it. I thought they'd arrested someone. Isn't he some kind of nutter? A serial killer, I heard."

"There has been an arrest, but I'd still like to ask you a couple of questions if I may."

"Sure, but I don't know what help I'll be. I was here when it happened."

"Did you know that Caroline was going to get engaged?"

"What did you say?"

"She was going to get engaged."

"Who to?"

"Danny Peterson."

I thought for a moment that the line had broken up, but then I realised it was the sound of laughter.

"Who told you that? Caroline wasn't going to get engaged to that loser. She only went out with him a few times then she gave him his marching orders."

"Do you know why?"

"She said he was a creep."

"Was she seeing anyone else?"

No reply.

"Josie? Do you know if she was seeing someone else?"

"Yes, she was."

"Who?"

"I don't know."

"It's really important, Josie. It may help to catch Caroline's murderer."

"I honestly don't know his name. The last time we spoke, she told me she was seeing someone. I'd never known her so happy or excited."

"Are you absolutely sure she didn't tell you his name?"

"He was married. That's why she wouldn't tell me."

I believed her, but I was pretty sure I *did* know who he was.

Graham Tyler's expression, when he saw me walk into the shop, confirmed everything I'd suspected.

Beth was busy with a customer, so I went straight through to the office, and closed the door behind me.

"How long had you and Caroline been having an affair?"

"Don't call it that." Tyler put his head in his hands. "You make it sound sordid. We were in love."

"Then why didn't you come forward after she was murdered?"

He looked up—there were tears in his eyes. "How could I? I'm married with a child. It would have destroyed my marriage."

From where I was sitting, he'd already done that all by himself, but this wasn't the time.

"How long had you been seeing Caroline?"

"For about three months."

"What about Danny Peterson? How did Caroline hide it from him?"

"Danny?" Tyler managed a half-laugh. "There was no

Danny. She'd dumped him before we got together. She thought he was a bit of a joke."

"Are you sure about that? Could she have been lying to you?"

"No! I'd have known. I loved her. "

Of course you did—just like you love your wife.

Chapter 23

"Hello, Danny." I stepped out of the shadows just as he opened the door.

"You scared me to death."

"Sorry about that." I'd been waiting outside his flat for the best part of an hour when his car pulled up.

"What do you want?"

"I have a question for you."

He unlocked the door. "I just want to forget all about it. I need to move on. I'm sorry."

"Just the one question, and then I'll leave you alone, I promise." I crossed my heart.

"What?"

"Why did you kill Caroline?"

The silence seemed to hang over us for an eternity, but I guess it was no more than a few seconds.

"You're crazy." He tried to slam the door in my face, but I pushed it open with ease. He went flying backwards and landed in the hallway in a heap. I'd cast the 'power' spell as soon as I'd seen his car arrive

"I'll call the police," he said, as he got to his feet.

"Be my guest. You can tell them how Caroline ended the relationship ages ago. How she thought you were a joke."

Danny looked as though I'd punched him in the stomach.

"That's a lie!"

"Not according to Josie Trent. You know Josie, right? Caroline's flat mate."

"How would she know? She's been out of the country for months."

"She and Caroline spoke on the phone."

"Josie's a liar. She always has been."

"Did Caroline tell you where to shove your engagement ring?"

"You don't know what you're talking about."

"She did, didn't she? But you wouldn't take 'no' for an answer, would you?"

"Get out of here!"

He raised his hands to push me, but I blocked him, and then threw him up against the wall.

"You asked her to marry you, and she said 'no'. Did she laugh in your face when you showed her the ring?"

"I loved her!"

"You strangled her!"

"I was only trying to make her be quiet. I had to make her understand how much I loved her. I would have given her anything, and I would never have cheated on her. She was seeing a married man. Did you know that?"

"I did actually. In fact I've just been talking to him. Was that the final straw, Danny? Couldn't you handle the idea that Caroline would rather have shared a married man than be with you?"

"You'll never prove it. The police have already charged Kilburn with her murder."

I took the digital recorder from my pocket, pressed 'rewind', and then 'play'.

"I loved her!"

"You strangled her!"

"I was only trying to make her be quiet."

"This had better be good," Kathy said when I arrived at her house. "Amber and Pearl were harder work than the kids."

"Sorry about leaving you in the lurch like that, but it was all in a good cause."

"I heard on the news something about another arrest?"

"Danny Peterson has been charged with Caroline Fox's murder."

"Hang on. Wasn't he your client?"

I nodded. "He was delusional. He'd convinced himself that Caroline Fox wanted to marry him even though she'd ended the relationship ages ago. He couldn't or wouldn't take 'no' for an answer. She was actually seeing someone else."

"How did you know he'd done it?"

"I have Amber to thank for that. When I saw her swollen finger, I realised it was similar to the injury on Caroline Fox's finger. Danny Peterson had tried to force the ring onto her finger. She laughed in his face and tried to pull it off. He lost control and strangled her. She managed to get one of her hands between his hands, and her neck, but it wasn't enough—he was too strong. The small puncture wound on her neck came from the diamond ring. After she was dead, he forced the ring back off her finger."

"How come the police didn't pick up on the fact that she was seeing another man?"

"Her new man was married—someone she worked with. Caroline and he had both kept their relationship under wraps. Even after she was murdered, her new man daren't come forward for fear of what it would do to his marriage."

"He should have thought about that before. I still don't understand why Danny Peterson came to see you in the first place."

"Even though his brother had given him an alibi, Danny was still worried the police might put two and two together and come after him. The so-called 'Animal' serial killer fiasco was a godsend for him. It made it look as though Caroline's murder was one in a series of murders. But the story was in danger of losing legs. He thought my involvement might be enough to resurrect it."

"What about the guy the police had already arrested. The serial killer?"

"There was no serial killer. That was just press talk. Pauline Lyon and Trisha Lamb were murdered by Derek Cairn — Trisha Lamb's brother. He'd been an extremely talented hairdresser in his heyday. He'd won awards and appeared to have a promising career in front of him. But then the drink had taken over. He'd already lost a couple of jobs because of his drinking. Trisha had been trying to help him through it. She must have thought the new job was a sign of better things to come, but then he was sacked again. He'd been drunk, and had made a total mess of Pauline Lyon's hair. She'd complained and Cairn was fired. That pushed him over the edge. He was so enraged at being fired that he tracked down Pauline Lyon and killed her."

"Why kill his sister though?"

"We may never know, but my guess is that Trisha had seen the artist's impression of the murderer's tattoo and realised it was her brother's. The eye witness had described two daggers through a heart when in fact it was actually a pair of open scissors through a heart. She probably tried to persuade Derek to hand himself in to the police. When he refused, she must have threatened to go to them herself."

"Wow! So you nailed both murderers. What did Maxwell say?"

"About what?"

"Don't be coy. About the small matter of you single-handedly solving all three murder cases for him?"

"I haven't spoken to him since the arrests, but I do have a meeting with him in the morning."

"Make sure you wear something sexy."

The next morning, I was in interview room three at the police station. Jack Maxwell, aka smiling boy, was seated opposite me. I'd taken Kathy's advice and dressed sexily—jeans and a baggy jumper.

"Nice décor," I said.

"Do you ever turn off the smartass?"

"Just making conversation."

"The stunt you pulled with Peterson was stupid."

"Getting him to confess, you mean?"

"A secret recording like that is inadmissible."

"Has he formally confessed?"

"Yes, but—"

"So why are you giving me a hard time?"

"I'm just saying. There are procedures to be followed."

"Those procedures weren't getting you very far were they? You'd charged the wrong man with three murders."

"Cairn has now been charged with the murder of Pauline Lyon and Trisha Lamb. Danny Peterson has been charged with the murder of Caroline Fox. Martin Kilburn will be charged with wasting police time, and

Peterson's brother has admitted he provided a false alibi. He will be charged in due course. "

"And?"

"And what? That's everything."

"I was waiting for the part where you say 'thank you'."

"I wouldn't hold your breath." He looked me straight in the eye, hesitated, and then said, "People like you are the bane of my life."

"People like me?"

"Private investigators."

"Do you have some kind of P.I. phobia?"

"They're a blight on society. Things worked out this time, but they don't always—take it from me. If I find out that you have interfered in any more of my investigations, I'll come down on you hard."

"If that's your idea of a 'thank you', I gotta tell you—it kind of sucks."

"And now, I want the name of your source inside the force."

"What source?"

"Don't try to be cute. There are things you couldn't possibly have known without an insider. Someone is feeding you information, and I want to know who."

"I don't have a *source* inside your *force*. You have my word on that."

He laughed. "And I'm supposed to take your word for it?"

"You can please yourself, but it's true."

"How do you explain how you knew about the puncture mark on Caroline Fox's neck? That information was never made public."

"I used magic."

"What?"

"Didn't you know? I'm a witch. Would you like me to show you? I could turn you into—"

"We're done here." He stood up.

"I suppose a reward is out of the question? Or a medal?" He glared at me. I took the hint. When I was halfway through the door, I turned to him and said, "And seeing as how you were wondering, I'm a great kisser."

His face flushed red, but before he could speak, I was out of there. What was I thinking? That wasn't like me at all. Still, the expression on his face had been worth it.

Chapter 24

I strolled into the office feeling on top of the world. Cairn and Peterson were behind bars, and word would soon spread about my involvement in their capture. Hopefully that would bring some new business my way. And to top it off, although Jack Maxwell hated P.I.s for some unknown reason, he apparently had the hots for me. Who would have thought it? I still wasn't interested — I didn't date asshats — at least not intentionally.

"Good morning, Mrs V," I beamed.

"Do you want the good news or the bad news?" she said, without looking up from her knitting.

I should have known it was too good to be true. "The good news?"

"The man came to repair the scratches on your desk."

"And the bad news?"

"That psycho cat attacked him."

"Where is he now?"

"In your office, but if I had my way he'd have been through that window."

"Not Winky. The man. The desk repair man."

"He left. He said he wasn't being paid enough to put up with a crazy, killer cat."

Great!

Winky was curled up on my still-scratched desk — fast asleep.

"What *is* wrong with you?" I yelled.

He opened his one good eye. "Do you mind? I'm trying to sleep."

"Oh? I'm *so* sorry. I didn't realise YOU WERE TRYING TO SLEEP!"

He jumped off the desk and scurried underneath. "What's your problem?"

"What's my problem? Hmm, well, let me see? *You're* my problem."

"What did I do? What has the old bag been saying?"

"You chased the desk repair man away."

"Desk repair man? How was I supposed to know that's who he was? I thought he was a thief. I was protecting your property. You should thank me."

"Jill, there's someone to see you." Mrs V's voice came through the intercom.

"Has the desk repair man come back?"

"Jill? Can you hear me? There's a man here to see you."

I was going to have to get a louder intercom — either that or knock a hole through the wall.

I walked through to the outer office.

"You need to get this stupid thing repaired." Mrs V thumped the intercom. "There's a man here to see you."

"So I see."

"I'm Dougal," the man introduced himself.

"Jill Gooder."

"Bugle."

"Nice to meet you Dougal Bugle."

He looked momentarily confused, but then smiled. "A joke?"

"Allegedly. What can I do for you?"

"We'd like to run an article on how you brought the 'Animal' serial killer to justice."

"There was no serial killer. He was a figment of your

paper's imagination."

"Could we maybe go into your office to discuss it?"

"Are you allergic to cats?"

"Cats?"

"Small, furry things with whiskers."

"No, why?"

"No reason. Why not? Come on through."

"Mr Bugle," Mrs V called.

"That's not actually my name."

"Would you like a scarf?"

He gave me a confused look.

I shrugged. "Just take one. It'll be easier in the long run."

"Any particular colour?" Mrs V opened the cupboard doors.

"Blue?"

"Sky blue, navy blue, turquoise—?"

"That one looks nice."

"There you go, then." She wrapped the navy blue scarf around his neck.

"Does she do that with all your visitors?" he asked, as soon as we were in my office.

"Mrs V? Oh yes. She's partial to a scarf."

"My last name is Andrews by the way."

"Not Bugle, then?"

"What happened to your desk?"

"*He* happened." I pointed to Winky who was underneath the leather sofa.

"What happened to him?"

"He didn't see eye to eye with someone."

Dougal looked at me blankly. Some people just don't get my sophisticated sense of humour. He went on to explain that he wanted to do an article on how I'd shown the local police force, and Jack Maxwell in particular, to be totally incompetent.

It was very tempting.

"I'm not interested in doing a hatchet job on the police."

"But they're incompetent. You have to know that."

"I couldn't possibly comment."

"The public has a right to know."

"If that's the article you want to write, then you can count me out."

"Okay no hatchet job, but I'd still like to do a piece on you. It will be good for business."

I certainly needed the publicity; those bills weren't going to pay themselves.

"I get to approve the article before publication?"

"Of course."

"Do I have your word on that?"

"You have my solemn word."

"Okay let's do it."

After the twins' overnight stay, it had taken me several hours to get the living room and kitchen back into shape. There were cups and plates everywhere, and they'd managed to trail crumbs all across the carpet. Every surface seemed to be covered in greasy fingerprints.

The worst was still to come—now I had to tackle the spare bedroom. They'd only spent the night, but it looked like a hurricane had hit the room. I should have persuaded Kathy to let them stay at her place. She probably wouldn't have even noticed the mess.

I stripped and remade the bed, dusted and polished every surface, and then vacuumed the carpet. I'd just about finished when I knocked the bedside cabinet with the vacuum cleaner. To my horror, the small glass angel figurine, which my adoptive mother had bought for me when I was eight, toppled off the cabinet and shattered as it hit the skirting board. Shards of glass were sprinkled all over the bedroom carpet.

I could still remember the day when she'd bought those figurines — one for Kathy and one for me. Kathy's had lasted no more than a month. I couldn't remember exactly what had happened to it; she was always breaking things. I crouched down and stared at the remains of the angel. I was on the brink of tears when I realised that all was not lost. I could use the 'take it back' spell to restore it. I loved magic!

I cast the spell, and lo and behold my treasured figurine was restored. I picked it up and gave it a gentle kiss.

"What the — ?" Kathy screamed.

I spun around to find her standing, open-mouthed, in the bedroom doorway.

"Kathy. I didn't hear you come in."

"What's going on, Jill?"

How much had she seen? How long had she been standing there? She must have let herself in while I was vacuuming. I stood up, figurine still in hand. "I was just tidying up after the twins. They're even more untidy than you." I forced a weak laugh.

"It was broken." She pointed at the figurine. "It was in pieces."

"Don't be silly. It had just fallen onto the carpet."

"I'm not stupid, Jill. I know what I saw. One minute, it was in a thousand pieces, and the next — " She pointed to the figurine. "What's going on? Tell me."

I cast the 'forget' spell, put the figurine back on the bedside cabinet, and said, "I didn't hear you come in."

Kathy stared blankly at me for a moment. "You were vacuuming."

"Is something up?"

"No. I just needed to escape from the kids for an hour." She glanced down at the figurine, and for a horrible moment, I thought the spell might not have been strong enough. "Anyway, I wanted to hear how you went on with Jacky Boy."

"He was his usual obnoxious self, what did you expect?"

"He must have been at least a little grateful for the way you cleared up those murders?"

"You'd have thought so wouldn't you?"

"He wasn't?"

"He basically told me to butt out of his investigations."

"Maybe he's just playing hard to get?"

"Or maybe he's just an asshat."

I ushered Kathy out of the bedroom, and away from the figurine. I didn't want to run the risk of it jogging her memory. I was going to have to start putting the chain on the door, so Kathy couldn't just walk in unannounced, or who knew what she might see.

We drank tea, Kathy moaned about Peter and the kids in a loving kind of way. I listened. She tried to persuade me that I should sign up for online dating. I told her to butt out of my love life—like I had one. After two hours, Peter rang to ask why it was taking her so long to buy a pint of milk. We hugged and she left.

I was really beginning to enjoy being a witch. Now

there's a sentence I never thought I'd say. My mother was right. I should spend more time in Candlefield where I'd have the freedom to be more open about who I really was. It's not like my time there would affect my old life because time would stand still in Washbridge while I was away. I wasn't sure if I wanted to work with the twins though—there was only so much stress I could handle. Perhaps, I could treat my time in Candlefield as a kind of break—a chance to recharge between cases. There was another advantage to being in Candlefield. I wouldn't have to put up with Mrs V and Winky. Barry, I could handle.

My phone rang; it was Aunt Lucy.

"Hi, Jill. How are you?"

"Fine thanks. Look, if it's about working in the tea room, I'm not sure it's for me."

"That's not why I'm calling. Grandma asked me to speak to you, although why she can't do it herself, I'll never know."

"Grandma?" This couldn't be good.

"She thinks you should have some help to learn the spells."

"It's okay. I seem to be mastering them. You have enough on."

"That's just it. She doesn't want me to help you; she plans to do it herself."

Huh?

"Jill? Are you still there?"

"Yeah. Sorry."

"Did you hear what I said?"

"Grandma is going to help me to learn the spells."

"Are you okay with that?"

"Err—yeah—I guess."
"Okay. Good. We'll see you soon then."
"Yeah. Soon. Bye."
Oh bum!

BOOKS BY ADELE ABBOTT

The Witch P.I. Series:
Witch Is When It All Began
Witch Is When Life Got Complicated
Witch Is When Everything Went Crazy
Witch Is When Things Fell Apart

AUTHOR'S WEB SITE
Http:www.AdeleAbbott.com

FACEBOOK
http://www.facebook.com/AdeleAbbottAuthor

MAILING LIST
(new release notifications only)
http:/AdeleAbbott.com/adele/new-releases/

Made in the USA
San Bernardino, CA
25 August 2016